THE WINTER
PHANTOMS

THE WINTER PHANTOMS

Angela Bull

A Dolphin
Paperback

This paperback edition published in 1995
by Orion Children's Books
a division of The Orion Publishing Group Ltd
Orion House
5 Upper St Martin's Lane
London WC2H 9EA

First published in Great Britain
by Dent Children's Books in 1993

A catalogue record for this book is available from
the British Library

Printed in Great Britain by Clays Ltd, St Ives plc

ISBN 1 85881 221 6

For Jimmy

CHAPTER ONE

'Are we nearly there?' asked Freddie, for about the sixth time.

No one answered. Mum was too intent on driving safely through the maze of dark, unfamiliar lanes to speak. Kit, sitting on the front seat next to her, simply stared ahead, unwilling to admit that he'd bungled the map-reading, and had no idea where they were. Elinor, who'd guessed Kit's mistakes, was too kind to say anything.

'It shouldn't take you much above an hour to get here,' Uncle William had boomed cheerfully down the phone, but the dashboard clock showed it was more than two hours since the Trenthams left home. Night had fallen long ago, and still the lanes twisted on; up and down, down and up.

'Well,' persisted Freddie, '*are* we nearly there?'

'Yes,' snapped Kit. 'And don't whine. It puts Mum off.'

'It isn't Freddie,' protested Mum. 'It's these roads that are putting me off. I'd no idea the Mill House would be so remote.'

'Stupid, isn't it?' responded Kit. 'Who'd want to be stuck out here, miles from anywhere?'

Kit liked towns. His idea of fun was meeting friends, going round shops and riding the escalators, intoxicated by the crowds and the loud music that flooded out of the stores. A lonely house in the wild hills did absolutely nothing for him.

'I don't know about stupid,' Mum answered reflectively. 'I suppose it suits Uncle William. He always wanted to retire to a house with an interesting history, and that's why he likes this old Mill House. I don't think being stuck out here will bother him a scrap.'

'Will it bother Aunty Fee?' asked Elinor.

'I don't expect so. She's very easy-going, you know.'

Elinor didn't really know. They didn't often meet up with Uncle William, who was Mum's mother's brother, and his wife, Aunty Fee, whose real name was Felicity. Occasionally Mum wrote to them, and a letter would come back, either in the great looping scrawl which seemed to match Uncle William's booming voice, or in Aunty Fee's neater script, always telling them about Uncle William's historical research on the Industrial Revolution, with its early mills and factories.

'Dead boring!' as Kit usually remarked.

This same research had finally taken Uncle William and Aunty Fee to the lonely stretch of moorland hills, in which the Trenthams – Mum, Kit, Elinor and Freddie – were so hopelessly lost, and, specifically, to the old Mill House, where the family was going to a New Year's Eve party.

'It's getting beyond a joke!' sighed Mum, as the car ground up a narrow lane between high walls. There were no lights, no houses; nothing but dark emptiness.

'Shall I sing?' suggested Freddie.

'D'you want us all to be sick?' snapped Kit again.

Elinor understood the snap. Freddie, their little brother, the tadpole with the enormous eyes and spindly body, had recently become a choirboy in a famous cathedral choir. Auditioning for it had been his own idea. He'd always loved singing. But his family, who'd taken the whole business with a large pinch of salt, were stunned by the enthusiasm with which the cathedral's music director had welcomed him.

He'd been singing on Christmas Day. Mum had switched on the television, and she and Elinor had watched Freddie's choir process through the candlelit cathedral in white ruffs and surplices. The music soared past towering arches and stained glass windows, and sometimes the cameras lingered on Freddie's small, earnest face, and huge, shining eyes.

'It's incredible! I'm shattered!' Mum murmured from time to time.

'Me too!' echoed Elinor.

Kit, very much withdrawn behind a new football annual, had been silent. He – the eldest, the cleverest – had had his nose well and truly put out of joint by Freddie's sudden rise to fame, and Elinor knew just how much he minded. But of course she didn't dare say anything. Kit would have been furious. All her life she seemed to have tiptoed round him; smoothing, praising or placating.

'I *want* to sing,' pleaded Freddie, from the back seat of the car.

'Just hang on a bit,' Mum answered, 'and let's concentrate on finding the Mill House. The party'll be over before we arrive, at this rate.'

Good, thought Elinor. Then they might be able to turn round, and go back to their nice ordinary house, in its nice ordinary street. Except that Uncle William had insisted on their staying overnight, so cases had been packed with their night things. Elinor knew she was the odd one out. Kit adored parties; Freddie was nearly as eager. She alone dreaded them. Kit had not nicknamed her 'Mouse' for nothing.

'I shall go on calling her Elinor,' Mum had said, when he first started the nickname.

'But Mouse suits her,' Kit had argued.

Like Freddie, Elinor was small, though her features were neater, and less striking, than his. Freddie's bright hair stuck up like a halo. Elinor's was combed back, and clipped into a little brown pony-tail. Kit was the only one to inherit the long limbs of their sailor father, who had spent Christmas neither at home, nor in a candlelit cathedral, but on a tanker in the Pacific, connected to them by a crackling phone, into which

3

Elinor had felt too tongue-tied to say more than, 'Happy Christmas, Dad,' and, 'Thanks for the clothes.'

He had sent her black silk, ankle-length culottes, and a white embroidered top, which he'd bought when his ship docked in Hong Kong. She was going to wear them at Uncle William's party. If they got there. If she had to. It would be so much more comfy to stay in her old jeans and sloppy sweater! Familiar things made her feel safe.

'Mouse wouldn't mind if the party *is* over when we arrive,' Kit announced teasingly, jolting Elinor from her thoughts.

'It'll be all right, Elinor,' said Mum.

Freddie came up with a new idea. 'Let's play I-Spy.'

'In the dark?' Kit sneered.

'We could spy things the headlights show up.'

They all looked into the bright beam, as it pointed ahead, and saw a tiny flake drifting through it. Then another, and another.

'Snow!' Kit was excited.

'Brilliant!' cried Freddie.

'That's all we need,' Mum groaned.

Elinor glanced towards her, between the headrests. She could tell from the droop of Mum's shoulders how tired and anxious she was.

'Aren't we nearly there, Kit?' she asked.

Kit switched on his pencil torch, and made a great thing of examining the map, which lay on his knee.

'Maybe two miles.'

He sounded as confident as ever. But was he really sure? Elinor wondered.

'Isn't that a signpost coming up?' she asked.

'Yes. We'll go left,' said Kit.

Mum slowed down, peering. 'It says Bellshill to the left, Kit. We went through Bellshill half an hour ago.'

'We're going round in circles!' squeaked Freddie. He alone was still taking an uncomplicated delight in their wandering journey.

'There's something wrong with this map,' muttered Kit.

'We'd better go straight on,' said Mum, releasing the brake.

'I know exactly where we should be going.' Kit sounded defensive, even though no one had accused him of anything. 'The Mill House is north-west of Bellshill, and we're coming from the south-east.'

'But the roads aren't straight. They're all twisty,' Freddie pointed out.

'As if I hadn't noticed, goof! The torch battery's going.'

'We'd better ask someone,' said Mum.

But there was no one to ask. The road wound on, rising and falling.

'Look!' Freddie's sharp eyes were the first to spot a light. 'A house, all by itself. I bet a witch lives there.'

'Of course there are loads of witches in these hills,' observed Kit.

'There might be.'

'And ghosts and goblins. You'd believe anything, poor old Freddie.'

'Would somebody ask here?' said Mum, stopping by the cottage.

'I'll go,' Elinor volunteered, before she realized what she was saying.

'No,' said Kit. 'I will.'

And Elinor, who'd gone mouse-shy at the thought of ringing an unknown doorbell, felt intensely grateful to Kit.

Still, she was glad she'd got out of the car. It was refreshing to stand in the open air for a minute. She'd begun to feel queer and disoriented as the road climbed and swung.

'You don't have to follow me,' said Kit.

'I'm not going to.'

She stood motionless by the roadside, as he walked

5

away. Snow softly touched her face, sifting down from the dark sky. Vast invisible spaces seemed to stretch around her. This might be the end of the world, she thought.

Immediately she was aware of a sound. It was rushing water, not far away. In the headlamps' ray she could see the road ahead humping as it crossed a bridge.

A moment later Elinor was leaning over the parapet, gazing down. Not that she could see anything. It was too dark. But the noise was awesome; thrilling. A deep river, in full spate, was leaping and tossing over the rocks in its bed.

Elinor shivered at the thought of falling in, and dug her fingers, for safety, into the loose stones of the parapet. They were big, rough stones, built into a mortarless wall.

And, all at once, her fingers touched something quite different; something smooth and circular, wedged deeply in. She wiggled, and the thing – whatever it was – came away in her hand; flat, round and solid. Kit suddenly joined her. Impulsively, Elinor dropped her find into her pocket.

'I was right,' Kit said. 'We cross this bridge, and then it's not much further.'

Elinor had no attention to spare for directions.

'Look at the river,' she exclaimed.

'It's pitch dark.'

'Sorry. I mean, listen.'

'Yes, well – wow!'

'It must be deep, mustn't it?' said Elinor eagerly.

'I'll say. Don't go falling in, Mouse. I'd hate to have to rescue you. There must be quite a current.'

They stood side by side in the falling snow, listening.

'Was there a witch in the cottage?' asked Elinor, breaking the silence.

'No. A bloke laying carpet tiles.'

They laughed together.

The car bumped over the bridge, and climbed another steep hill. Kit pored over the map, his torch genuinely flickery.

'There should be a sharp bend. Yes – here it is.' He tried not to sound surprised. 'Now we turn right.'

The lights picked out a gap in the wall.

'Down here?' groaned Mum, for a thread of lane dropped steeply back down the hill, pocked with stones and furred with snow.

'Go on. Bottom gear,' Kit encouraged. 'The Mill House should be on the left. This'll be the drive.'

They turned between sturdy gateposts, and bumped along a track cut like a shelf in the hillside. Where the ground fell away on their right, a house loomed beneath them. They edged forward, parallel to its upstairs windows, with a peaking, dipping roof not far above them.

'I've never seen a house so close to a hill before,' said Freddie.

'There'll be a bit of a gap for ventilation.' Kit knew everything. 'I expect there'll be a little path between the house and the hill. A sort of mouse track.'

Exhilarated at having brought his family to their destination, he grinned at Elinor in the torchlight.

'Don't call me Mouse in public,' she begged.

'Help!' Mum burst out.

The drive suddenly swung, in a steep, slippery comma, down to a flat stretch of ground at the far end of the house. Other cars stood about, powdered with snow. Their car skidded, then ground to a halt.

Kit leaped out. 'I'll get the cases.'

Elinor sat and stared at the house. Lights gleamed dully behind drawn curtains, and a brighter lamp shone above the door. That was all she could make out in the snowy darkness.

The front door opened, and Uncle William surged

towards them. He was a large man, with a shock of hair and enormous spectacles.

'I thought I heard a car. We were getting worried when you were so late, especially since the snow started. Christopher! Elinor! Frederick! Alison, my dear, how are you?'

'Pretty exhausted,' said Mum. 'This really is the back of beyond.'

'We like it, though. Fee! The Trenthams are here.'

He led the way into the house, an arm around Mum. Kit and Freddie followed with the suitcases, and Elinor came last, clutching her party clothes in a carrier bag.

A passage stretched before them, running the length of the house to a distant staircase. Candlelight glowed from open doors, and groups of guests milled around with glasses in their hands. There seemed to Elinor a disquieting sense of the party having gone on for a long time already, and of their being interlopers, not wanted. Unfriendly eyes seemed to watch their progress along the hall. Shadows wavered overhead.

Elinor clasped the smooth round object in her pocket for comfort.

'Sorry it's rather dark,' Uncle William apologized. 'Fee likes candles at parties. Fee! Where are you?'

Aunty Fee sailed up the hall from behind them, wearing a long skirt, with a lot of dangling, jingling jewellery.

'Lovely to see you, dears—'

She didn't finish her sentence. Mum, swinging round quickly, as if to greet her, seemed to trip, and fell awkwardly, crashing her head against the newel post at the foot of the staircase.

CHAPTER TWO

They clustered round Mum where she lay on the floor, her face drained of colour, her eyes shut.

'Is she dead?' wailed Freddie.

'No; no, of course not. Look, she's coming round.'

Mum's eyes opened. She half sat up, putting her hand to her head. 'What happened?'

'Just a fall, dear,' said Aunty Fee. 'I'm afraid you tripped over the rug, and gave your head a nasty crack. Does it feel bad?'

'Splitting.'

'We'll take you upstairs,' Aunty Fee went on. 'You can lie down till you feel better. I'm sure you'll soon be all right.'

She put an arm round Mum, and began to help her up the staircase. Uncle William bustled after them, carrying Mum's bag; and guests, who had rushed forward to help, moved away.

Elinor climbed the stairs, her knees weak with fright. She had been too far back to see exactly why Mum had fallen, though she supposed Aunty Fee was right about the rug. But it was strange. Mum wasn't usually the sort of person who fell over things.

Kit and Freddie followed her silently. Mum was helped into a bedroom; the door was closed. Even Kit stood blankly, not knowing, for once, what to do.

Then Aunty Fee reappeared, smiling.

'There's nothing to worry about. She'll be fine when she's had a bit of time to recover. Let me show you your rooms, dears, and then you can get yourselves ready, and come down. Boys in here. This is your room, Elinor.'

It was a square bedroom at the farthest end of a long landing, which doubled back through the house, above the hall. Elinor reckoned that if she pulled back the curtain, and peeped out, she'd see their car parked in the falling snow. Ridiculously homesick already, she blinked back a tear. If only they'd turned round, when they first got lost!

She plunged her hands miserably into her pockets, and touched – well, what was it? She pulled out the object she'd found among the stones of the bridge, and, for a moment, forgot her dismay in sheer astonishment.

The smooth round thing looked as if it was made of gold. Perhaps two inches across, with an odd little knob inside a loop at the side, it lay, real and solid, on her palm, not spoiled or tarnished by its time in the wall. But gold, she remembered, didn't tarnish or rust.

Examining it more closely, she saw something like a hairline crack, running all round the circumference. She dug in a thumbnail – and jumped, as a thin lid sprang up, revealing a creamy dial, set with hands and Roman numerals. It was a watch; an old-fashioned pocket watch, in a gold case. The little knob was, no doubt, the winder, enclosed in a ring by which it could be hung from a watch-chain. Elinor seized it, trying to make it turn, but the knob was stuck fast. The two slim, arrow-headed hands pointed immovably to 6.20 on the creamy-ivory face.

Instinctively she knew it was old. It was the sort of watch a television actor would consult in a costume drama. The way the lid flew open and shut was fascinating. She wished the hands would move as easily. She tried the winder again, but without success. 6.20, it insisted; 6.20, and nothing else.

Never mind. It seemed a strangely comforting thing to hold. She'd always liked something small and solid to cling on to, when she felt anxious or afraid. Kit teased her about a lucky pebble she'd kept for years; indeed, only the fear of his scorn had stopped her from bringing it to the party. The watch would do instead.

Freddie banged on her door. 'Are you ready?'

'Nowhere near.'

'We are. We're going down.' He sounded excited. 'See you.'

'Don't duck out of it, Mouse,' Kit ordered sternly.

Chance would be a fine thing, she reflected, as they hurried away. She laid down the watch, and opened the carrier bag. Unexpectedly, changing her clothes helped her. The person she saw in the mirror was so far from the Elinor she was used to, she might have put on a disguise. The culottes fell to her ankles like a floor-length dress. Her grandmother's locket, lent by Mum for the occasion, gave an old-world touch to the new blouse. And when she'd removed the clip, and brushed out her brown hair, it spread gracefully – prettily, even – over her shoulders. No longer everyday Elinor, modern Mouse, she was suddenly a girl from a time past.

She took a deep breath, and opened the bedroom door.

Shadows seemed to rush up the landing towards her; shadows full of gloom and horror. They circled her, pressing against her. Alarmed, Elinor drew back, slamming the door.

Don't be so crazy, she told herself. The landing's empty. She could even hear music from the party, drifting upwards. All the same, it was a relief to pick up the gold watch, and slip it into the pocket of her culottes. She felt better then.

Steeling her nerves, she went out again, and down the stairs, only to find there was nobody left in the hall. The guests had gathered in a big sitting room, where beams laden with holly crisscrossed the low ceiling, and the light from candles and a log fire threw pale glimmers over half-seen faces. Someone was playing blues on a saxophone; a melancholy wail of sound. Freddie, she noticed, had crept close to the piano. Kit perched on a windowseat, displaying his handsome profile against a crimson velvet curtain. She noticed one or two other children – a boy in a kilt, a girl with glasses – but she avoided them, and sank quietly on to the hearthrug.

'Superb!' boomed Uncle William, as the saxophone sobbed into silence. 'Freezes your guts. Now then.' He laid a heavy hand on Freddie. 'Here's young Freddie Trentham. I bet most of you saw him carolling his heart out on Christmas television. Are you going to sing for us, Freddie?'

'OK,' Freddie answered promptly. 'I'll do *I saw three ships*. And I shan't need a piano.'

Though she knew he could sing, Elinor's nerves tightened. Kit stared frostily into the distance. Utterly unfazed, Freddie opened his mouth, and a sound as clear as crystal rang through the room. The effect was electric, the applause rapturous.

'Big-headed little show-off,' Kit muttered in Elinor's ear. He'd wormed his way to the hearthrug.

You can't be big and little together, Elinor wanted to say. But she didn't argue with Kit.

'Something else!' voices clamoured.

'I shall be sick.'

And, for once, Elinor rounded on Kit. 'Don't be so mean. He has got a gorgeous voice.'

Instantly, she regretted it. The look Kit gave her showed that he was seriously displeased. Without another word, he stalked back to the windowseat. Of course he'd expect her to apologize, and admit that his judgement was right. What a terrible party! She still felt upset about Mum's fall, and now Kit was being awkward about Freddie. Torn between her feelings for both her brothers, Elinor clenched nervous fingers over the watch in her pocket.

'*The Holly and the Ivy*,' somebody called to Freddie. There was a rustle of approval round the dim room.

Glancing furtively towards Kit, Elinor saw that a girl she hadn't noticed before was with him, bending forward and whispering. Girls often liked Kit, and this one must have detached herself from a group at the far end of the room, to speak to him.

In the flickering light she looked very slender, papery, almost weightless. She wore a long, dark dress, and a mass of pale hair hung down her back, in curling, tangling locks. She whispered urgently, gesturing with hands as thin and white as bones. Amazingly, Kit took no notice, and presently the girl drifted back into the shadows.

Freddie had already begun to sing.

'The holly and the ivy
When they are both full grown—'

Elinor looked up. Both holly and ivy were festooned along the beams, garlanded with loops of scarlet ribbon. The shiny leaves sparkled in the flame-light. The berries hung like drops of blood.

'If you please,' a low voice murmured, and a hand touched Elinor's arm, ice cold through her sleeve.

Elinor stifled a shriek. The girl who had been talking to Kit had somehow circled the room, and reached her. For the first time Elinor saw her face. It was white as mist, with strange, greeny-grey eyes that were wide with fear.

'Is something the matter?' Elinor exclaimed in a whisper. Her thoughts flew to Mum.

'Can you help me?' murmured the girl. 'I can't find my brother, Tom.'

'I'm sorry,' Elinor whispered. She truly was. 'But I'm afraid I don't know anyone here except my own brothers.'

Total despair clouded the white face, so that Elinor too was alarmed.

'Have you asked Uncle William?' she questioned.

The girl drew back. 'I don't speak to *him*!' she answered sharply.

'Oh.' Elinor was puzzled. 'Well, I suppose I could help you to look for your brother if you want me to, but it's difficult when I've never met him.'

'Thank you. I knew you'd help me, as soon as I saw you. I'm so worried; so dreadfully worried.'

And, at that moment, *The Holly and the Ivy* came to an end. People clapped – and suddenly the girl wasn't there.

'Supper next!' called Aunty Fee from the doorway. 'It's all on the kitchen table, and there's masses, so pile up your plates. Why don't you children set us oldies an example? Would you lead the way, Freddie, and you, Elinor, and Angus. Just across the hall.'

Electric lights made the kitchen another world from the dim sitting room. Elinor blinked, wondering where the girl had gone. But Freddie was beside her, beaming happily at the sight of so much food.

'Wow! Just look at all that!'

'Don't have too much,' Elinor warned him, for Freddie had been known to make himself sick.

'I won't. All the same . . .'

People behind pushed them forward. Somebody handed out plates. There were prawn parcels, tandoori chicken legs, asparagus rolled in ham, vol-au-vents bursting with mushrooms. Elinor felt giddy with so much choice. In no time her plate was loaded.

'There you go.' A helpful hand dolloped salad all over it.

She found Kit beside her. 'Oh, Kit, d'you know who that strange girl was?'

In her anxiety, she'd quite forgotten she'd meant to apologize to him.

'What strange girl?'

'The one who was whispering to you, just as Freddie was beginning on *The Holly and the Ivy*.'

Kit shrugged. 'I dunno. I don't remember. I know that's Angus over there.'

'The boy in the kilt?'

'M'm. Bit of a poser, isn't he?'

'Hasn't your little brother got a wonderful voice?' gushed a woman nearby.

Kit made a rapid get-away.

'I've just peeped at your mother, and she's fast asleep,' Aunty Fee told Elinor. 'So that's good. Now, find yourself somewhere to sit down while you eat all that. Uncle William will get you a drink.'

Elinor moved into the hall, looking up and down its length. Admirers had penned Freddie in the kitchen, perilously close to the tempting table. Kit, back on the windowseat, was blocked off by chattering people, whom Elinor didn't like to squeeze past. Another door led to a dining room, formal and stiff, where elderly ladies had their heads together in serious conversation. Elinor retreated, and tried a third door. This, clearly, was Uncle William's study, with mounds of books and papers on the table. Elinor backed out, and stood still, plate in hand. A dull ache of tiredness, or worry, or some inexplicable gloom oppressed her. The ceiling was too low; the shadowy hall too sinister. The plate of food, which she didn't want, weighed her down.

Suppose she just went to bed? Would it be very rude? Would it be, as Kit would tell her, sickeningly mouse-like?

She approached the staircase, which rose to a window halfway up, and curled round to the black, unlit landing above. She wished Aunty Fee would turn on the lights. Laying her plate down on a small table, she searched for some switches, but there didn't seem to be any.

'Oh! I've found you. I'm glad.'

The girl was suddenly there beside her.

'Hello,' Elinor said. Her heart was beating fast at the shock of the girl's appearance, and the embarrassment of being discovered alone. People at parties were meant to laugh and chat in a jolly crowd, not creep about in corners.

But the girl seemed equally anti-social. 'I'm glad you're by yourself. I wanted to tell you, I think I know where Tom is.'

'Oh, good!' Elinor responded, as heartily as she could.

'No.' The white face clouded again. 'It isn't good. I'm afraid he's been locked in the stable.'

'Locked in the stable?' Elinor echoed.

'Yes. I want to go and see him, but . . .' She shivered.

'It sounds rather frightening,' said Elinor.

'It is. Would you – come with me?'

'Me?' Elinor was overwhelmed with horror at the prospect. She tried to be brave. 'Well, I will if you want me to. But I shan't be able to do anything.'

'Just come,' begged the girl. 'This way. Quick, before they find we've gone.'

There was a door, hidden behind the staircase. The girl opened it, and they plunged out into the freezing night. Snow no longer fell, and the ground sparkled under an icy moon.

'It's so cold!' exclaimed Elinor. Her clothes might have been made of tissue paper.

'What does cold matter when poor Tom's suffering?'

Elinor had no answer for that. She closed the door behind her, and found she was on the narrow track which, as Kit had predicted, ran between the house and the hillside. A mouse track – and she felt distinctly mouse-like. On her right, the house loomed, as silent and dark as if the whole chattering party had been extinguished. A snowy bank climbed upwards on her left.

The girl darted forward, and Elinor hurried after her. Steps appeared, cut into the bank. They scrambled up, and on to the drive. Snow had covered the tyre tracks, leaving the drive a ribbon of pure white.

'Mind your dress.' The girl scooped hers up, so that the hem wouldn't get wet.

Doesn't she realize I'm wearing culottes, Elinor wondered, slipping and sliding along.

'Over there!' The girl pointed to a huddle of out-buildings, beyond the end of the house. They clustered, low-roofed and unlit, where the hill sloped less steeply. The girl flew between them, and stopped beside a rough stone wall, where there was a window, blocked by a grating. Elinor, catching up, saw her peering through the bars, which she grasped with cobweb hands.

'Is he there?' the girl whispered anxiously.

Elinor peered too. Moonbeams struck through the grating into a small, crooked stable, where a figure lay, spreadeagled on the straw.

'That's him!' The girl's breath caught in a sob. 'Tom! Tom, it's me, Susanna.'

The person inside groaned, struggled to his feet with a rustle of straw, and moved towards the grating. With no clouds to obscure the moon, Elinor could see that he was a boy not much older than Kit, though taller and stronger. His hair was tousled, his shirt torn, and his face was all streaked and crusted with blood.

'He hurt you!' gasped Susanna.

'Thrashed me with his riding whip.' Somehow Tom managed a rueful laugh. 'But don't mind, Susanna. I shall survive. It was good of you to come.'

'I had to. Tom, what had you done to anger him *this* time?'

Tom's words came tumbling out in a passionate rush. 'How can you ask, after what you saw this morning? I told him how terrible it was that Isaac Corby had drowned at the stepping stones, and that he shouldn't allow children to cross the river at such a dangerous place. He should do something to help them – but, naturally, he won't.'

'Oh, Tom, I can't bear it.' Susanna was weeping. 'When you were still away at school, I used to dream of your being here with me. I thought it would save me from loneliness. But it's all gone wrong.'

'Well, at least I *am* here, much as I hate the mill and all that goes on there. We have our moments together.' He smiled at her, affectionately but lopsidedly, through streaks of dried blood. 'Don't linger here, Susanna. It's bitterly cold.'

'I can't go back and join Uncle William's merry-making as if nothing had happened; not when he's treated you like this.'

'*Uncle William?*' Interloper though she felt in this shattering scene, Elinor had to interrupt. 'You don't mean it's Uncle William who's beaten Tom?'

Susanna swung round. 'Of course it was Uncle William. He's a monster!'

The force of her anger seared through the night. Elinor jumped back in alarm, and then a sudden cloud blew across the moon, hurling down a sharp flurry of snow. The wall, the grating, Susanna herself were lost in a stifling cloak of blackness.

'Where am I?' cried Elinor, gasping for breath.

She swung round, stretching out her hands into the blizzard, and saw behind her pale squares of window, which must belong to the Mill House. Susanna, Tom, the drowned child who had somehow brought trouble on Tom, were too much to cope with. She fled for shelter, speeding through the snow to the light.

Car doors banged. Voices called good night. Elinor was back on the flat sweep of ground where Mum had parked. Uncle William stood, square and solid, just outside the front door.

'Mind how you go!' he called cheerily, as a car scrabbled and scrunched up the sharp bend in the drive, and vanished along the top side of the house. 'And a happy New Year!'

How could he sound like that, when he'd just beaten poor Tom, and locked him in the stable?

Elinor dodged, unseen, behind him, slipped into the house, and upstairs.

CHAPTER THREE

Elinor surfaced from a night of bad dreams, to hear strange bumps and thumps from somewhere beyond her bedroom. It took a moment before the fuzz of nightmare cleared from her brain, and she remembered that she was at the Mill House, and that last night there had been the party, which had ended with the visit to the stable.

More thuds from the landing. They were, she realized, the heavy footsteps of people carrying something. A man's voice – not Uncle William's – grunted, 'Careful!' A faint moan. An exclamation which might have come from Kit. Something awful was happening. Elinor cowered, mouse-like, under the bedclothes.

Below she heard doors – the front door, perhaps a car door – open and close. There were no cheery calls of goodbye. An engine revved. Elinor sprang out of bed, and swept back her curtains. An ambulance was moving off, negotiating the steep twist of the drive, and disappearing along the back of the house.

Tom!

Someone – Aunty Fee? – had found him dying in the stable, and dialled 999. Elinor sank into bed, her heart racing.

After a few minutes, she looked at her watch; not the gold one whose hands were stuck, but her ordinary wristwatch. *Ten past ten!* How could she have slept so long? Why hadn't Mum come in, as she usually did? Elinor scrambled out of bed again, dressed rapidly in her old, familiar clothes, and combed her hair neatly into its brown pony-tail. Back to everyday Elinor, who was going home this morning. Thank goodness!

Briefly she glanced out of the window once more. The snowy ground dipped into a steep valley, and rose on the far side. The Mill House, crouching on its shelf, was the only house in sight. Just a few dark walls, and tangles of trees, broke the blank whiteness, which lay, spread out, under the heavy grey sky.

Elinor, used to living among a crowd of houses, shivered at such cold isolation.

When she came out of her room, the landing, studded with closed doors, stretched gloomily towards the stairs. She found the bathroom, and then ventured uncertainly down to the kitchen.

Kit was there, eating cereal at the table, while Aunty Fee loaded the dishwasher from the chaos of party plates and cutlery. There was no Mum, and no Freddie. Thankfully, there was no Uncle William either.

'Well, you really are a dormouse,' said Kit, looking up, spoon in hand. 'You snored through the lot.'

'What lot?'

'Freddie being sick, and Mum going to hospital.'

Elinor sank on to a chair by the table. 'Hospital?'

Aunty Fee turned round, trying to smile, and look unruffled. 'Don't worry, darling. It'll be all right. But she was rather ill in the night. Her head ached dreadfully, and she had a bit of a temperature. So I called the doctor, and she thought that your mother should have a few days in hospital. It's called being "under observation".' She gave a little laugh which was meant to be reassuring. 'You probably heard the ambulance men clumping downstairs with the stretcher. They didn't like our drive! Anyway, it'll only be for a few days, as I said, so Uncle William and I will keep you three here. Then you can visit her. You mustn't look so upset, dear. It's only a precaution.'

'And Freddie ate too much, and made himself sick, the pig! That's why he's stayed in bed. Tandoori chicken always gets to him,' Kit remarked.

'Where's – Uncle William?' Elinor asked, through stiffened lips.

'He went down to the hospital as well, to see your mother settled in. He's going to buy you some odds and ends for while you're here.'

And Tom – ? But suddenly, he didn't matter. Not like Mum. Elinor's eyes filled with tears.

'Hot tea for you.' Aunty Fee bustled round kindly. 'You're bound to feel the shock.'

'I didn't say goodbye.'

'Oh, Mouse, you'd only have cried,' said Kit. 'Anyway, I'm going to bag Mum's bedroom, so that I don't have to be in with Freddie. It was disgusting how sick he was.'

Elinor sipped the hot tea, into which Aunty Fee had put a spoonful of sugar, and it did help a bit. But she still felt shattered by the news about Mum; and, at the back of her mind, the question lingered – where were Tom and Susanna?

'Isn't this kitchen dark?' said Kit. He never minded offering his opinion on other people's things. 'But then it's bang up against the hill.'

'There's a path outside the window,' said Aunty Fee. 'Narrow, but enough to give a bit of light and air.'

'A mouse track. I guessed that. I was right!' Kit declared triumphantly.

Elinor remembered how she had run along that path with Susanna. Before they found Tom.

'It's a strange house,' Aunty Fee went on. 'They must have had a job building it, when the hillside's so steep. But it was put here for the family who owned the mill in the valley below. The river comes racing down, you know, and long, long ago it powered an old mill. There was a waterwheel, Uncle William says, which drove the machinery. The millowner lived here, and there were cottages in the valley, I believe, for the mill-workers. They've all vanished now.'

'A waterwheel! How primitive can you get?' exclaimed Kit.

'Well, remember it was nearly two hundred years ago. You've got to think of water power, candlelight, horses in the stable for transport—'

'I wonder if it was the same river we saw,' Elinor put in quickly. She didn't want to think about stables. 'We stopped by a river, on the road from Bellshill. We couldn't see it, but it sounded—'

'Terrific!' interrupted Kit.

Elinor was glad of the interruption. She'd been going to say 'scary'.

'It was the same one. You can go down the hill and look at it, if you like,' said Aunty Fee. 'But don't risk the stepping stones. They'll be lethal in the snow.'

'Oh!' Elinor cried sharply.

'What's wrong?' asked Kit.

'Nothing.'

She couldn't say, in front of Aunty Fee, that Tom had blamed Uncle William for a child drowning at the stepping stones.

'It was because Uncle William got so interested in the mill and its history that we came to the Mill House,' Aunty Fee told them. She had finished loading the dishwasher, and was putting glasses in a bowl of soapy water. 'You know how he loves history. But sometimes I wish we hadn't come.'

'Why?' asked Kit.

'It's lonely,' said Aunty Fee; and then, almost as an afterthought, 'and it's a sad house, somehow.'

'It's certainly dead peculiar,' said Kit.

Breakfast was over, a wan Freddie had been visited,

and Elinor and Kit had gone out into the snow. Because Elinor had no proper coat with her, Aunty Fee had lent her a cloak to keep her warm; a thick, hooded, woollen cloak, which fell nearly to the ground. Kit had his own bomber jacket. They had climbed the steep twist of the drive from the front door, and were standing at the corner, where it levelled out along the back. Snow had slithered down from the roof, leaving the gutters fringed with icicles, and covering any traces of footprints that Elinor and Susanna might have left on the path below.

'Incredibly primitive, but I suppose a crumbly old millowner wouldn't be particular,' said Kit.

'There's a nice view at the front,' Elinor ventured.

'M'm. Bleakish. Are you OK now?'

'I'm coping. Will Mum be all right, Kit?'

'Sure to be. Observation just means keeping an eye on her, not rushing her to the operating theatre or anything. She'll be fine in a day or two.'

How could he sound so confident? Elinor had lived through the funeral several times already.

She looked the other way, towards the stables. They sagged and tottered, oddly decrepit in the morning light. Kit followed her glance.

'That's where the pool table is,' he remarked.

'What pool table?'

'One that Uncle William put in the old stable loft. Angus and I went out there after supper, and had a game. That's why we weren't around.'

'Weren't you?'

But all the party, after Susanna had appeared by the staircase, was a blank to Elinor.

'Angus was the guy in the kilt,' Kit explained.

'You said he was a poser.'

'He was OK. I beat him.'

'Kit,' Elinor began, making up her mind to confide, 'did you hear anything when you were playing?'

'Like what?'

'People talking – or groaning.'

'Groaning? What *are* you on about, Mouse?'

'You remember the girl with long hair, who spoke to you while Freddie was singing?'

'I don't, actually. I remember you said something about her, while we were getting supper.'

'Yes. Well, when we'd got it, I didn't know where to go to eat mine. I tried the dining room, and Uncle William's study, and I didn't feel comfy anywhere. I didn't want all that food either. So I'd just made up my mind to go to bed—'

'Oh, Mouse!' jeered Kit.

'When this girl suddenly came up, and told me that Tom, her brother, was locked in the stable. We went out to see. It was dreadful, Kit. He'd been beaten up, really badly. Blood, and that. And who d'you think had done it?'

'Jack the Ripper.'

'You've got to be serious, Kit. It was Uncle William.'

There was a pause. Kit stared at her. 'I don't believe you.'

'It's true. Tom said so.'

'Uncle William? Come off it. He couldn't. He's too old, and – soft.'

'He did.'

'You were dreaming, Mouse.'

'I wasn't. I'll show you. Tom may still be there, locked up.'

She began running over the frozen snow, towards the stables. They were even more ruinous than she'd expected. Walls had tumbled into heaps of stone; snow-crested rafters pointed jaggedly upwards. Only one bit was roofed and whole, with garage doors open, and the tracks of Uncle William's car curling away.

'That's where the pool table is.' Kit indicated the window above the garage. 'Now, what about this stable, or person, or whatever?'

'I don't know,' said Elinor slowly. Nothing looked as it had done in the moonlight.

'I was right. You were dreaming. Silly old Mouse! Let's go down to the river.'

I wasn't dreaming, thought Elinor, as she followed him. It really happened. Dreams fade away into a dark blur, but every detail of her experience with Susanna and Tom remained sharp and clear. She could still see Susanna's tragic face and pale hair, and the way her thin hands clasped the bars. She remembered exactly how Tom had struggled to his feet, and smiled lopsidedly through the grating.

'Have we any cousins, or relations, called Tom and Susanna?' she asked.

'I dunno. I've never heard of any. Come on. This way.'

Kit disappeared round the stables. A track fell precipitously downwards, between stone walls. Each stone was outlined in snow.

'I'd love a sledge!' called Kit from below.

'It's too bumpy for sledging.'

'Only on the path. We could go down the fields. Or we could get skis.'

'We don't know how to ski.'

'Stop being so pathetic, Mouse. We'd soon learn. I would, anyway. Everyone says it's easy.'

He charged on. Elinor followed, her cloak flapping.

Suddenly, through the quiet of the shut-in valley, her ear caught again the sound of water; descending, pounding, roaring. Kit gave an excited shout. The ground levelled out, and they found themselves on the very brink of the river.

Some gnarled and ancient holly trees, twined with ivy and splashed with scarlet berries, stretched their crooked branches over the rushing mass of water. It came hurtling down from the hills, bouncing and leaping over the stones, in waves that were as black as ink against the snow-crusted banks.

'Some river!' breathed Kit.

Elinor simply clung to one of the holly boughs.

'Look – the stepping stones,' said Kit, pointing.

Sure enough, there they were, a little way upstream; a dozen humpy rocks, making a pathway over the water. They were piled with snow, and they glittered where ice had frozen to their sides.

'It'd be fun crossing,' said Kit. 'Dangerous – but I bet I could do it.'

'You'd be mad!'

Kit poised himself on the bank, as if to jump, but Elinor wouldn't look. She began to run back up the hill.

Kit came crossly after her. 'I could have done it. I'll do it some time. You'll see.'

After that, she and Kit were somehow at odds for the rest of the day. It was a pity, because Elinor longed to talk about Tom and Susanna, but Kit wouldn't take the subject seriously, so she gave up trying. All the same, she kept wondering where they were; and she made quick, furtive attempts to find them, opening doors when no one was about. But there was no trace of them, and she almost thought that Kit was right, and that the whole strange experience had been a dream.

In the end, the cosiest thing was to sit with Freddie. He was well enough in the afternoon to be propped up with pillows, and play Patience on a tray.

'Black ten goes there,' Kit pointed out, wandering in.

'I can see, thank you very much,' Freddie grumbled. 'Isn't Kit a pain?' he confided to Elinor, as Kit sauntered away.

'Not really,' answered Elinor, as she always did when Freddie made similar remarks. Belief in Kit, and loyalty to him, went very deep in her. She could remember enjoying so many things with him when they were small.

'I hope Mum's better soon,' sighed Freddie, tiring of cards.

'Oh, so do I!' echoed Elinor, glancing from the unfamiliar bedroom to the cold, white hills outside.

CHAPTER FOUR

'You can take turns to visit your mother; one each day,' said Aunty Fee at breakfast next morning. 'They say she needs rest, and one of you at a time will be enough. We'll go by ages, so it'll be Kit first. *If* we can get out.'

More snow had fallen in the night. When she had looked out, Elinor had been seized with panic at the thought of being trapped. On an impulse, she had dropped the old gold watch into her jeans' pocket. Kit wouldn't know, and it was comforting when it bumped solidly against her hip.

The three Trenthams and Aunty Fee went out into the cold, muffled in an odd mixture of outdoor things which Aunty Fee provided, to shovel a way through the drive to the lane. Gradually they cleared a narrow passage, throwing up ramparts of snow on either side. Small avalanches slid down the bank, filling the mouse path, and pressing threateningly against the dark wall of the house. When Aunty Fee's car, with Kit looking smug in the front seat, nosed cautiously away between the gateposts, Elinor half wondered if she would ever see them again. Suppose she and Freddie were stuck for ever at the Mill House.

With Uncle William.

He hadn't helped to clear the drive. He suffered from what Aunty Fee called 'a tricky heart', so he was safely shut away in his study, and wouldn't, Elinor hoped, come out till teatime.

'What d'you want to do?' she asked Freddie, after

27

they'd returned to the house together. Freddie had drifted into the sitting room, and was warming his hands by the fire.

'We could play cards,' he said.

'OK. What game?'

'Snap.'

But just as they were in the middle of it, with Elinor letting Freddie have a good share of the wins, Uncle William's large spectacles, and larger face, peered round the door.

'That looks fun!' he exclaimed jovially. 'Can I join in?'

'If you want,' said Freddie.

So a third chair was pulled to the table, and Uncle William hurled himself doughtily into the battle.

'What a treat,' he purred. 'I haven't played cards since I was a boy.'

But his presence made Elinor decidedly uneasy. She couldn't forget Tom, and the dark stable. It was dark in the sitting room too. Snow wreaths, piled on the window ledges, dimmed the daylight. Thickly garlanded evergreen leaves – more black, in fact, than green – snaked round the beams and over the fireplace. The shadowy walls enclosed a room which seemed very far from home.

'Snap!' bellowed Uncle William, his enormous hand crashing down on a pair of aces – the hand that had wielded the riding whip.

'I don't much like this game,' protested Freddie, as his last cards were swept away.

'Not like it? I thought everybody loved Snap. It's just the thing for a winter's day.' Uncle William shuffled eagerly, ready to deal a new round.

Elinor jumped to her feet. 'It's not snowing, and you haven't seen the river yet, Freddie. Come on. Let's go out.'

'I have to steer clear of the hill, with my heart trouble,' said Uncle William regretfully.

Well, we've got *that* to be thankful for, Elinor reflected. She pulled on Aunty Fee's thick socks and wellies again, and threw the woollen cloak round her shoulders.

'It's funny,' remarked Freddie, as they closed the front door behind them. 'I thought I'd want to stay in, after all that shovelling. And then I didn't.'

'I can do without Uncle William,' said Elinor.

'I don't mind him,' said Freddie. 'He's like a big, bouncy dog. It's the house, I think. It sort of squashes you.'

'I know what you mean,' agreed Elinor.

They slid and floundered down the hill. Below them, the chatter of the river grew louder and more triumphant, as if it was celebrating its freedom in the silent, snowbound valley.

Elinor scooped up a snowball, and aimed it at Freddie.

'Don't!' he squeaked, so she threw it at the wall instead, where it spattered in milky drops.

'Kit would have thrown it at me,' said Freddie. And then – 'Was Kit arguing with somebody yesterday, when I was in bed?'

Elinor thought back rapidly. She and Kit had had a few brushes, but she couldn't really call them arguments. After all, she nearly always gave in quickly.

'I don't think so,' she said. 'Why?'

'I heard these angry voices. One of them sounded like a boy.'

'The wind?' suggested Elinor hopefully. 'There! Look!'

They had reached the straggling belt of ancient hollies. Beyond them, the black river rushed and swirled. Ice floes were swept along in its waters, and there were icicles hanging from the projections of the stepping stones, and from low holly boughs which caught the spray.

'Isn't it *deep*?' Freddie darted to the river's edge.

'Take care!' She suddenly wished she hadn't brought him. 'Don't get too close. It's slippery. Hang on to a tree, like me.'

She'd grabbed a holly branch for an anchor with one hand – a scraggy branch, with a few, dull leaves. Her other hand was in her pocket, gripping the smooth circle of the old watch.

Luckily, Freddie was sensible enough to grasp a branch too; but, just as she noticed this, her eye was caught by a movement beyond him. Someone was coming towards them. She couldn't tell who it was, since, even as she looked, the trees were unaccountably thickening from a withered straggle to a dense cluster. All at once there seemed to be more trunks, more leafy boughs, more glowing berries.

Elinor gasped. For a moment everything seemed to sway in and out of a thin white mist. Then she saw Tom – she was certain it was Tom – threading his way through the hollies. She recognized his broad shoulders, and wiry brown hair.

'Freddie,' she whispered urgently. 'D'you see that person?'

'Yes,' said Freddie, not very interested. His attention was fixed on the racing, skipping water.

So it hadn't been a dream. Tom *was* real. A dozen baffling questions spun through Elinor's mind, but she ignored them, and looked at Tom instead, her fingers tight on the old watch.

All the marks of blood had gone, and he was walking briskly, though with a hint of stiffness. He wore a brown skirted coat, and a pair of long boots, and he had a coil of rope over his arm. He stopped about twenty metres upstream from them, whistling gently, and studying the holly boughs above his head; and his eyes shone very blue in a face that was both thoughtful, and bright with enjoyment. He looked as if he was pondering over a scheme which pleased him a lot.

'D'you think ducks ever come here?' wondered Freddie.

'M'm. Probably lots of them.'

'Only they might freeze. There's tons of ice under the banks.'

Tom took an end of rope, and tossed it neatly over a branch. He grimaced slightly, as if the movement hurt.

'What d'you think he's doing?' whispered Elinor.

Freddie glanced towards Tom again. 'Tying a rope to a tree.'

'I can see that. But why?'

'I dunno.' He shivered. 'We've seen the river now. Let's go back.'

'You go ahead. I'll stay a minute longer.'

It was awful how, suddenly, she was eager to be rid of him.

'I've just thought,' said Freddie. 'If Uncle William's back in his study, I could get the cards, and play Streets of Paris by myself.'

'Good idea.'

'I've never got Streets of Paris out. Kit says he has lots of times.'

'I bet you will today. Go on. Don't hang about getting cold.'

Freddie moved off at last, his matchstick legs, ridiculous in overlarge boots, struggling through a mound of snow.

'Walk in our footprints,' called Elinor. 'See you.'

She looked back at Tom. He seemed to have two ropes, not one. He had fastened the second to an adjacent branch, tugging on the knots to tighten them. The rope ends curled down in spools to the bank. Now he gazed across the river, as if measuring the distance. Near his feet, the snow-capped stepping stones reared through the inky current.

Satisfied, apparently, he left the ropes, and headed

upstream through the trees. Some instinct, which she couldn't quite understand, drew Elinor after him. She wanted to know more about him. Not that she meant to speak to him; she was too mouse-shy for that. But she felt impelled to follow, to watch him, and find out what he was doing.

As they came out of the trees, she saw that, on both sides of the river, the hills curved back, leaving space for clusters of cottages. Well, not cottages exactly. Hovels, was the word that sprang to Elinor's mind. They crowded in two dismal huddles, facing each other across the black water; some on the near bank, some beyond the stepping stones.

Tom walked on, unperturbed, giving a long, shrill whistle. Rickety doors opened; small heads popped out. Children.

'I'm back!' called Tom. 'I'm starting on the job. But you needn't help unless you want to. It's Sunday.'

But they did want to help. They scrambled out into the snow, and went after him, in a hopping, hurrying flock, as if he was the Pied Piper.

They passed between the hovels, and came to a large, squarish building, beyond them all, which stood in a walled yard, at the very edge of the river. Elinor felt almost certain it was the mill, even though Aunty Fee had seemed to think it had vanished. Slipping between the dingy cottages, she hovered outside the yard wall, watching.

Tom strode boldly in through the gate, and made his way to a woodstack. He began lifting down lengths of timber, and measuring them against each other, setting the longest on one side.

The children gathered round, with shrill, excited cries.

'Hey, get that 'un, mester.'

'Nay, t'other's bigger.'

'Try yon.'

A little girl, bent double over the wood, pointed. Tom smiled at her, lifted the end of the plank – and still the little girl was bent. She was like a right angle, inside her tattered cape. Horrified, Elinor realized that the girl couldn't stand straight.

As she gazed more intently at the children, shock followed shock. Some were limping on rough, home-made crutches. Others lurched unsteadily on crippled legs. Backs were bowed, or bent sideways. Limbs were as thin as twigs. Their clothes were dreadful too. More than one went shoeless in the snow. Several had bare arms and legs emerging from ragged garments. Some wore sacks pinned round them, by way of coats.

Elinor had seen films of disasters on TV, but this was happening in front of her eyes. Here were actual children, misshapen and half starved. Yet, despite their wretchedness, there was a wild gaiety about them. They called and shouted to each other. They tugged at the planks in an effort to be helpful, and cuffed each other with playful ferocity.

Snowballs were flung.

'Hi, stop it!' shouted Tom, as one hit him.

There were shrieks of laughter.

The more she watched, the more baffled Elinor became. If it hadn't been for the reassuring solidity of the watch, which she still gripped in her pocket, she might have believed that the whole strange scene was a dream.

Nothing about the situation seemed to worry Tom. He hoisted the longest plank on to his shoulder – again with that swift grimace – and, while the children eddied round, stretching frail arms to help or hinder, he moved away out of sight, towards the spot where he had tied the ropes.

Suddenly, startlingly, Susanna was beside Elinor. She was muffled in a cloak not unlike Elinor's, with long strands of pale hair blowing out from under the hood, and greeny-grey eyes staring hauntingly from her white face.

'Where's Tom? Isn't he here?' she asked.

'He was, a moment ago,' said Elinor. 'He's taken the children along the river. He was carrying a plank – I don't know why.'

'Ah!' A glint of pleasure lit Susanna's face. 'That's good.'

'What's he doing?' asked Elinor.

'Making a bridge.'

Of course he was! The ropes, the planks – it all added up. She recalled Tom's passionate words in the stable.

'Because of the child who was drowned at the stepping stones?'

'Yes; Isaac Corby. He lived with his grandmother on the far side of the river.' Susanna gestured towards the cottages on the opposite bank. 'His parents are dead, like ours.'

The sorrow in her voice was chilling. Elinor didn't know what to say. A mother in hospital, a father on a tanker, were nothing in comparison.

'I reached the river myself, just after they'd pulled Isaac out,' said Susanna. 'I was taking some coffee for Tom. He goes out long before breakfast. I found him on the bank, with two men from the mill. At first I didn't know what they were bending over. Then I did . . .' Her voice trembled, and she was silent for a moment. 'Tom tried to bring Isaac round,' she went on. 'He knows how such things can be managed. Our father was a doctor, and he taught Tom a great deal before he died. But it was too late. Isaac was dead. It seems he'd overslept. Children do. He must have been hurrying over the stepping stones, fearing he'd get the strap for missing time. And then he slipped. Someone heard him scream. Tom ran and pulled him out, and the other men ran too. He'd been washed against the

34

bank. A drowned child! I saw his wet hair, all plastered over his face . . .'

'How awful!' exclaimed Elinor. 'No wonder Tom wants to make a bridge.'

'Yes. It's very important. That bridge is a sign that Tom's on the side of helping and caring for people, not treating them cruelly. But he's got to believe that himself. I'm worried that he feels he's become part of the evil already, by working at the mill, but Uncle William gave him no choice.'

'Evil?' questioned Elinor.

'Yes. It *is* evil to make children work such long hours. Tom has endless quarrels about it with Uncle William.'

Those arguing voices Freddie heard, thought Elinor, startled.

'Doesn't Uncle William think it's evil?' she asked.

Susanna gave a short laugh. 'He shuts his eyes to bad things. He only wants to get rich, as fast as he can. When Tom finished at school, we both thought he could start to train as a doctor, but Uncle William wouldn't spare the money for it. And it's useful for him to have Tom working for him here.'

Her eyes flashed with such anger, that Elinor stepped back involuntarily, thinking she had never met anyone like Susanna. And it wasn't just her passionate way of speaking, and her unexpected appearance. It was her deathly pallor too, her strange air of weightlessness, and, of course, her clothes. A long brown dress rustled under her cloak, which fluttered sideways in the breeze to reveal clumsy, square-toed shoes with buckles, such as Elinor had never seen before, and thick woollen stockings, wrinkling baggily round the ankles.

'Tom's trapped,' Susanna went on, desolately. 'If he can't train as a doctor, he'll never escape from this terrible place, any more than Isaac did.'

The wind sharpened, shrieking down the valley, and

snatching away Susanna's miserable words. It snatched at her cloak more fiercely, and at the powdered snow, blowing it up between the two girls in a dizzying spiral of white.

Elinor's own cloak billowed up over her face, blinding her. She had to let go of the watch, and use both hands to free herself from the muffling folds; and instantly she was attacked by a volley of snowflakes, flung at her in a stinging, freezing blast.

She fled for the nearest shelter, while the wind hustled her along, screaming and moaning in her ears. She reached the wall, still marked by the snowball she hadn't thrown at Freddie, and crouched under it, dabbing the snow from her eyes.

When she looked back, Susanna had gone, and a whirling blizzard hid all the valley from her sight.

CHAPTER FIVE

The magazine Kit had brought her from Bellshill lay unread in Elinor's lap. She stared into the fire, turning the strange adventure over and over in her mind. Who *were* Tom and Susanna? Where did they eat and sleep? Who were the children, forced to work for Uncle William? The situation in the valley seemed as dire as it was puzzling, but who could she talk to about it?

Not Kit. He'd come back from the town in a restless, edgy mood; not at all in a state for listening to her problems. There was Freddie, but he was busy and happy with a new Lego set, and she couldn't bring herself to upset him. Aunty Fee? Well, Aunty Fee was nice, but, as Uncle William's wife, she was hardly a suitable person to confide in. Uncle William himself was, naturally, impossible.

'I'm talking to you, Mouse,' she heard Kit say irritably.

'Oh! Sorry. What?'

'I was wishing I hadn't bought you that mag. You don't seem very interested in it. I could have got another for myself instead.'

'I do like it,' said Elinor hastily, flicking over a page, and trying to lose herself in coloured pictures of winter fashions; proper winter fashions – 501 jeans and baggy jumpers – not dresses whose hems brushed the snow under fluttering cloaks.

The dim, lamplit room pressed in on her, as the unseen snow pressed on the windowpanes. Crowding armchairs lurked like monsters. Burning logs hissed and whispered.

A movement across the room made her jump. For a second, she thought she glimpsed a gesture of frail hands, parting the curtains. Pale hair gleamed, as a girl leaned towards the window, watching and waiting. Was it Susanna, looking out for Tom? Elinor's fingers tightened on the watch in her pocket, and then relaxed. A draught – surely only a draught – had rippled the velvet curtains, so that reflections of firelight had wavered over their glossy surface. That was all, that must be the explanation.

A draught, because Aunty Fee had come in, and gone out again. She was restless too. She picked up a newspaper, and put it down again; murmured something about soup on the Aga which ought to be checked, about making sure Freddie's bedroom was warm. She hurried away with her head tilted back, as if she needed more air to breathe.

Uncle William drowsed behind a heavy book. Freddie, sucking butterscotch, built up his Lego model. Aunty Fee and Kit had shopped generously that afternoon.

But all the presents in the world couldn't ward off

Elinor's worries, or the despair and frustration, which seemed to hang in the room.

'You'll never make that balance,' Kit told Freddie. 'And do you have to scrunch your butterscotch in such a disgusting way?'

'Isn't it lovely that Mum's feeling better?' Preoccupied though she was, Elinor rushed in automatically to keep the peace.

'You don't have to listen to me,' Freddie told Kit. 'And I know what'll balance.'

'You don't. See! I was right.'

Kit laughed derisively as Lego showered on to the table. Freddie, rather pink, began to build it up again.

'I do know how to do it. I might be an engineer when I'm grown up.'

Somewhere a door slammed. Aunty Fee, or. . . ?

'It was so brilliant, being back in a town,' sighed Kit. 'Bellshill's got everything. Smith's, McDonald's, video shops, one of those places for astral games. Who'd be stuck in a dump like this?'

'It's very—'

Uncle William cut across Elinor. His owlish eyes blinked over the top of his book.

'You seem discontented, Christopher.'

'Just dead bored. There's nothing to do here. If we were at home, there'd be loads of parties, and stuff.'

'Children nowadays are spoiled,' pronounced Uncle William.

Kit shrugged.

'Suppose you were a piecener,' Uncle William went on. 'Pieceners were child workers in the old mills,' he explained, as Kit looked blank. 'Suppose you'd been standing at a machine smoothing thread for the man who worked it, until your fingers were like polished bones, and your legs as crooked as a pair of tongs from standing ten to twelve hours a day.'

'Hey! Just suppose!' mocked Kit.

Crooked legs? What did Uncle William mean, Elinor wondered. Was he talking about the children who slaved for him, down at the hidden mill?

The logs in the fireplace rustled and muttered. The snow, the dark walls, closed them round. No wonder Kit had enjoyed the freedom of Bellshill! She wanted to tell him she knew how he felt, but he'd picked up his things, and was making a haughty exit, his heavy-lidded eyes scorning them all.

Next day it was Elinor's turn to visit Mum. Escape! she thought, as Aunty Fee's car ploughed gallantly through the lanes towards Bellshill.

'There's a house!' she exclaimed. It might have been the one Kit called at.

Aunty Fee laughed.

'Do you think it's dreadfully lonely at the Mill House?'

'It is, a bit.'

And not only lonely; sinister too. But Elinor didn't say that.

'I agree it's lonely,' said Aunty Fee. 'But William loves it. So there we are.'

A jolt. They were crossing the bridge where she'd found the old watch. It was in her pocket now. Somehow she seemed to need it all the time.

'Look! Three houses in a row!' Aunty Fee pointed excitedly.

They laughed together.

'Aunty Fee,' Elinor began carefully, 'who are Tom and Susanna?'

'Tom and Susanna? I don't think I know them.'

'They were—' Elinor broke off. She'd been going to say they were at the party, but of course Tom wasn't. She changed her words. 'They were relations of Uncle William's, I think.'

'Quite possibly. I don't know half his family,' said Aunty Fee. 'They're scattered all over the place. But we've only been married for five years.'

'Is that all? I can't remember when you weren't married.'

'We were a pretty ancient wedding couple. I tease him about all the things he used to get up to, before I met him.'

Elinor sighed. It was impossible to confide in Aunty Fee when it meant saying things against Uncle William. They drove on in silence, until Aunty Fee began asking what Elinor liked to do at home.

At last a hospital sign appeared, and Aunty Fee slowed down. 'I'll drop you here, and do a bit more shopping. Freddie must have some proper wellies. He's swamped in the ones I gave him. We'll get your things later. In you go, and look out for the direction boards. It's a big place. You want Ward 14. See you later.'

Mum lay in bed, wan, but recognizably herself. There were three other beds in the bay, so Elinor didn't like to say too much; but at least she could ask the main question that worried her.

'D'you know Tom and Susanna, Mum?'

'No. Who are they?'

'Could they be cousins? Susanna's around my age, and Tom's older. They call Uncle William, Uncle William.'

Mum frowned, thinking. 'I don't remember the names, but my brain's still horribly muzzy. How did you hear of them?'

'Susanna – just Susanna – was at the party.'

'You should ask Uncle William,' suggested Mum.

'OK.'

It was clearly no use pursuing the subject. Mum looked tired.

'Are you happy at the Mill House?' she asked.

'Yes.' What else could she say, under the circumstances?

'I always thought Uncle William was very nice.' Mum's eyelids drooped, so that, luckily, there was no need for even the briefest, vaguest answer.

The three other ladies in the bay snoozed peacefully, lulled by scents of Dettol and chrysanthemums. Radiators hummed, passing shoes squeaked on the nonslip tiles, distant trolleys rattled, yet all was drenched in calm tranquillity. Not like the Mill House. Why did the snowy light, which poured harmlessly through the hospital windows, glower so menacingly in the valley?

I wish Mum would hurry up and get better, so that we could go home, sighed Elinor.

'I don't really understand why I fell,' said Mum, opening her eyes, and speaking as if Elinor had been questioning her. 'It must have been because I was so startled when that girl appeared from behind the stairs.'

'What girl?'

'Thin, long-haired, pale. Yes, it was her dreadful, ghastly paleness that shocked me so.'

'I thought you tripped over the rug,' said Elinor. Her heart was beating fast.

'M'm. But I tripped because of the fright. One minute she wasn't there; then she was. Oh, I dare say I'm talking nonsense. Everything's mixed up in my head. Don't take any notice, darling.'

'Yes, OK,' said Elinor, smiling to hide the chill that had seized her.

'Look!' Mum brightened up. 'Here's Aunty Fee, with *more* flowers. Isn't she an angel?'

'Boots for Freddie!' Kit exclaimed indignantly. 'Boots for Mouse too, and a new skiing jacket. Chocky-bickies, yum-yum I *don't* think. Newspapers. Where's my sledge?'

'What sledge?' asked Elinor, as she gathered up the shopping she had spread out over the kitchen table at the Mill House.

'Honestly, Mouse, don't you remember anything? When we went down to the river, I particularly said I wanted a sledge. I was relying on you to ask Aunty Fee for one.'

Why didn't you ask her yourself, yesterday? The question was on the tip of Elinor's tongue, but she bit it back. It was fatal arguing with Kit when he was cross already.

'We could try with the big wooden tray,' she suggested; 'the one Freddie used when he was playing Patience in bed.'

She didn't really want to go out again. The daylight was fading, and a nipping wind blew. But poor Kit had been stuck at the Mill House all day, with just Freddie and Uncle William.

'I suppose we could. OK. You get it, Mouse.'

She might have known it would be hopeless. A tray, with squared corners and no means of steering, was *not* much of a sledge. It bumped, it stuck, it slithered into drifts. Kit fell off, and was crosser than ever.

'You're so selfish! You only got what *you* wanted in Bellshill!' he shouted.

Near to tears, Elinor clutched the watch in her pocket. Like her lucky pebble, it gave safety and comfort.

A cold sun sank, staining the snow with its long red rays. Kit stumped back up the hill to the house. Elinor stayed behind deliberately, letting him go, looking the other way.

Suddenly, in the gathering dusk below her, a tiny light bobbed among the hollies. Voices, faint as bats' squeaks, reached her ears.

Elinor propped the tray against the wall, and, chilly though she was, crept towards the river. How thickly the trees were growing! Their thorny leaves snatched at her new skiing jacket. She pulled a branch aside, and saw two small children, a girl and a boy, trudging towards her from the direction of the mill. They carried a candle in a little pot, whose feeble glimmer served to guide them through the thicket.

Tattered garments flapped from their bent and bony shoulders. Loose clogs chafed the heels of the girl, while the boy had only strips of sacking bound round his feet. He clung to his sister, his face drawn with pain and exhaustion.

' 'E belted me wi' 'is strap. 'E belted me wi' 'is strap,' he wailed, over and over again.

'Hush 'ee now. 'Tis done,' soothed the girl.

' 'E 'it me. 'E belted me wi' 'is strap.'

They passed close to Elinor. She smelled the bitter poverty of their rags, and of their starved and filthy bodies. On they trudged, limping and whimpering, their shadows wavering in the thin candlelight. Elinor stood for a moment, watching till the trees swallowed them up. And then she turned and fled, with the old watch digging into her hip as she ran.

CHAPTER SIX

Elinor charged at the steep hill, scrambling and stumbling, and forcing herself on, till the lights of the Mill House came into view. Then she slowed to a walk, her lungs heaving, her heart pounding.

Who *were* these people she kept seeing – Susanna, Tom, and the maimed and ragged children? Why were they here? As she paused outside the front door, a suspicion she had been trying to ignore could be held back no longer.

43

'Ghosts!' she whispered. 'They're ghosts!'

The crouching house and the snowbound valley swarmed with them.

She felt dizzy with fear. All around her in the gloom, unseen presences seemed to crowd and jostle, thrusting themselves between her and the door, demanding her attention. She spun away, panic-stricken, on the point of flying back down the hill; but they were there too, muttering and whining along the cold whisper of the wind, cutting off her escape.

Her heart lurched, and terror ran down her spine, like the groping touch of chill fingers.

'Help!' she cried, in a little mouse squeak. 'Help!'

Nobody came. She stood rooted to the spot, while a dim sky wheeled above her, and times past and present meshed together in a net, which trapped and held her.

'I can't bear it!' she moaned faintly – and was aware of instant relief at the sound of her own voice, weak though it was. At least it proved that she was alive, and herself, even if these bewildering things were happening to her. Before her, the Mill House rose squarely, with only a wall separating her from Kit and Freddie, Aunty Fee and Uncle William. The collar of her new skiing jacket snuggled round her neck; familiar gloves encased her hands.

As she made herself focus on these things, her heartbeat steadied. The ghosts couldn't harm her, she reminded herself; and calmness began to edge back, removing the haunting presences to a little distance. She half wondered if there might not be, after all, a perfectly reasonable explanation for her strange experiences.

She drew a deep breath, clenched her fists, and screwed up all her courage. Deliberately, she turned away from the house, and headed for the stable where Tom had been imprisoned. There was just the faintest chance that she might have overlooked something real and solid, when she and Kit had gone to investigate the ruined outbuildings; some place where a modern person might just have been shut up. And if there was, she was going to find it, and stop scaring herself silly over phantoms.

She switched on the light outside the garage, so that its yellow brightness shone over the bare rafters and crumbling walls she had seen before. No; there was no stable with barred window, where a boy could have lain, stretched out on the straw. None. She knew, with total certainty, that she must have visited it with Susanna in some time outside her own. Ghosts' time.

If she went down to the river, she'd only find the last remains of a holly grove which had flourished when Tom and Susanna were alive. Upstream, the land would lie empty where the mill and cottages had once stood.

Panic snatched at her again. It was too frightening, too inexplicable. Biting, unfriendly gusts of wind buffeted her through the gaping holes in the walls. She must go inside and tell someone. Kit. . . ? If she could get him on her side, as her ally, it would be wonderful! But he'd demand proof of the ghosts, she was sure he would; and she sighed with despair.

There was one more thing she could check. She switched off the garage light, and, on legs which felt like jelly from cold and terror, crossed to where the drive ran along the back of the house. Below lay the mouse track she'd used with Susanna. Drifts of snow filled it, but Elinor hurried along above it till she reached the tall staircase window, dimly lit from inside. There should be a doorway nearby, through which she and Susanna had passed.

But there was not. The wall stretched unbroken from the window to the corner of the house. For a moment she stood, staring, as frozen as the icicles which hung from the roof. Then she fled inside the Mill House.

The ghosts were there too; she felt them. As she closed the door, pausing in the dim hall passage, sadness seemed to well out of the shadows, folding itself around her. The air was thick with past sorrows; Tom's frustration, Susanna's despair. Elinor found herself doing what Aunty Fee had done the night before; tilting back her head to breathe, gasping, and fighting back a new surge of fear.

Keep calm, she told herself. You don't need to go over the top, just because you've seen some ghosts. It feels a bit stuffy in here after the cold outside. That's all.

Hanging her skiing jacket on a hook, she opened the kitchen door. Aunty Fee and Freddie were at the table, sugaring mince pies.

'Hello, darling. Are you frozen?' inquired Aunty Fee. 'I heard Kit come in, but I guessed you must be really enjoying the sledging to stay out so long.'

'Oh! The tray!' exclaimed Elinor. She'd left it down the hill, leaning against the wall. That outing with Kit seemed light years ago.

Aunty Fee didn't mind. 'I don't often use it,' she said. 'You can fetch it in the morning. Freddie and I will have supper ready in about half an hour. He's a super cook, you know, and he sings to me while I'm stirring.'

Freddie was humming, as he perched on a stool, carefully sifting sugar over golden-brown pastry lids.

'If I can't be a musician, I might be a chef,' he told Elinor.

'You were going to be an engineer yesterday.'

'I could be all three! I could be anything in the world!'

In his excitement he powdered the table with sugar. There seemed to be no ghosts in the kitchen. Maybe happiness drove them away. And because it seemed wrong to spoil the warm atmosphere, Elinor held on to her secret.

'Where's Kit?' she asked instead.

'I'm not sure,' said Aunty Fee. 'Try the sitting room.'

Elinor crossed the dark hall passage, and found Kit alone, hunched in the depths of a chair; and gloom, or ghosts, spread their chilling net again.

It was suddenly too much to face. Losing her nerve, Elinor backed out, but Kit called to her before she had shut the door.

'What are you doing, Mouse, coming in and out? Can't you make up your mind?'

'Sorry. I'm just going.'

'No, don't. I want you. Mouse, what have you been up to? You stayed out in the snow a heck of a long time.'

She was a mouse with Kit; she knew she was. Something about the arrogant stare of his heavy-lidded eyes paralysed her, as the stare of a cat paralyses real mice. But, in spite of that, she desperately needed his support, and her words came out in a half-reluctant rush.

'I've – been seeing ghosts.'

He frowned, then laughed. 'You remind me of Freddie, and the witch in the cottage. A guy laying carpet tiles, as it happened, and not a broomstick in sight. So what are these ghosts?'

She couldn't mention Tom and Susanna at once. An odd sort of loyalty demanded that she protected them from a possible sneer.

'Children,' she said. 'Poor little children, who slaved away at the mill in the valley; all thin and bent from working such long hours, and dressed in rags.'

'H'm.' He eyed her disbelievingly. 'Let me see, what TV programmes have you been watching recently?'

Tensed up as she was, and fighting back panic, this was the last reaction she needed. Suddenly, she was furious. 'It's nothing to do with television. It was what I saw just now, down by the river, after you'd stormed off in a rage.'

47

'Well, thanks for that, Mouse. Very kind, and charmingly put, I must say. So by leaving you to sulk, I missed out on a psychic treat? Well, well!'

'Actually,' she snapped, exasperated into boldness, 'you've seen a ghost yourself. The girl at the party.'

He smiled, cool and superior. 'Oh, yes. The invisible girl you keep going on about.'

'She wasn't invisible. She seemed so real, I'd no idea till now that she was a ghost. I'll explain, Kit, if you'll listen. D'you remember the morning after the party, when I was looking for an old stable near the garage?'

'Yes. You thought there was somebody there who'd been beaten up by Uncle William. That was a laugh.'

'There was, but— Oh!' The truth flashed through Elinor's mind. The Uncle William who had beaten Tom was not *their* Uncle William, so large and comfortable, with his spectacles and fondness for card games. It must have been an Uncle William of long ago. The two identical names had knotted her up, and now, as the knot untangled itself, her fear of the real Uncle William melted away, leaving her weak with relief.

'I was wrong about one thing, Kit,' she began again. 'It wasn't our Uncle William. It all happened in the past; I don't know when. I've been seeing the ghosts of two people who once lived here, as well as the mill children. They were a brother and sister called Tom and Susanna. They lived with their uncle, and he was very unkind to them. They were dead miserable, Kit. I can feel their unhappiness. It's in the air all around us, sort of dark and freezing. You can't get away from it. Don't you feel it too?'

She heard her voice rising shrilly, as disbelief set in hard lines over his face.

'Cool it, Mouse,' he advised. 'I'm beginning to think you're a touch jinxed, you know.'

'OK!' she cried. 'Think that, if you want.'

And she shut the door on him.

She stood in the passage outside, her pulses racing, as they always did after a confrontation with Kit. He was so powerful! And then, all at once, she knew she had been powerful too. She hadn't stayed to argue, to beg him to believe her. She'd walked out. On Kit! She'd never done anything like that before.

New confidence flared inside her, driving back the ghost-ridden gloom that filled the hall. She swung round, and did something which, a mere five minutes ago, would have horrified her. She walked straight to Uncle William's study, and opened the door.

'Hello, Uncle William,' she said.

He was seated at a large table, elbow-deep in papers. 'Supper ready?' he asked, all eager to get up and go.

'Not quite. Uncle William, can I ask you about something?'

'Of course. Ask away.'

'I want to know about the mill in the valley, and the children who worked there.' Not Tom and Susanna just yet.

Uncle William beamed with delight at her interest. 'Well!' he said. 'Take a chair, and I'll see what I can tell you briefly. There was indeed a mill, powered by a waterwheel. Its machinery spun raw wool into fine yarn. During the winter, when the river was full – like it is now – things worked nicely. The wheel shaft drove the machines at high speed, so that the workers had a job keeping up. But in summer, when the river ran low, things weren't so good. No energy supply, you see. That's why steam power took over from water. Only it wasn't easy to bring coal up a steep, lonely valley like this – not when you think how bad roads were – so a coal-fired boiler wasn't a good proposition here. Eventually, the mill closed, and the workforce was transferred to Bellshill, where coal could be got without too much difficulty.'

'I see.' Elinor pondered this short history for a moment. 'When was the mill working?'

'Around 1820, give or take a dozen years each way.'

'And the children?'

'That's a sad story, Elinor. You see, the men who minded the machines wanted help, to keep them going; not skilled help, just a nifty pair of hands. Children's hands would do, and children didn't need high wages. So lots were employed, on starvation pay, to stand by the machines all day, helping to string out the wool. They might start when they were as young as six or seven, and they worked from dawn till dusk. It was more than their poor little bodies could bear, often enough, when you think how tired and under-nourished they'd be. But if they dozed off, or fainted, they'd be beaten. It's not a pretty tale.'

'Who owned the mill?'

'The same man who had this house built; William Kershaw. He was born in 1780, and he was shrewd enough to latch on to machinery when it was starting up, and plenty of other people still used spinning wheels and handlooms. He set up his mill with its new machines, and he jerry-built some dreary cottages for his workers. Then, when he could afford a bigger and better mill, with steam power, in Bellshill, he packed up and went. The old mill fell into ruins, which people pillaged for stone, and now there's nothing left to show there ever was a mill at all.'

Except the ghosts, thought Elinor.

And then they heard Aunty Fee calling cheerily from the kitchen.

'Come on, everyone. Supper's ready.'

Elinor lay awake for a long time in bed that night, listening as the wind shrieked and shuddered down the valley. How icy those poor ragged children must have been, when winter closed in on them. Nobody had cared, except Tom; and somehow his caring, and their misery, together with Susanna's fears and anxieties, had been compounded into a mixture strong enough to last nearly two hundred years.

A picture flashed into Elinor's mind of Tom, whistling and smiling, with the ragamuffin pack hobbling round him. She found herself treacherously wishing that he, not Kit, had been her brother. If she'd gone to Tom with a story of ghosts, she was sure he would have listened sympathetically. Which was an odd thought when he was a ghost himself!

And he wouldn't have called her 'Mouse'. Alongside her anger with Kit for not believing her, a new determination was beginning to form. She wouldn't go on behaving like the timid little creature the nickname suggested; that must be left in the past. She wouldn't be labelled, or patronized, or put right by Kit any longer.

Somehow, the fact that the ghosts had revealed themselves to her, and not to him, encouraged her to be strong.

She went down to breakfast next morning in a resolute mood. Her brothers were already sitting at the kitchen table. Freddie, ominously pink, was letting a spoonful of golden syrup dribble over the edge of his bowl of shredded wheat, while he stared indignantly at Kit. Kit was putting on the charm.

'I'm incredibly good at carring shopping bags, Aunty Fee, and I can always understand the weirdest parking meters.'

'But it's my turn to see Mum on my own,' protested Freddie.

'Well, naturally I wouldn't expect to see Mum. I know it's Freddie's turn.' And, as Freddie relaxed, scooping drips back into his bowl, Kit directed his charm towards Elinor.

'Hi, dormouse,' he said pleasantly.

'I'm not a dormouse.'

It was a feeble retort – she'd need to practise! – and gave Kit the chance to lean back in his chair, smile, and remark, still pleasantly, 'Actually, I have a feeling that a dormouse isn't a proper mouse. Just a little furry rodent of its own species. Ever so sweet.'

She could have thrown something at him, but it seemed more dignified to ignore him, say hello to Aunty Fee, and sit down at the table.

'Kit's wheedling me into taking him to Bellshill today,' said Aunty Fee.

'Not to see Mum. I'm not trespassing on Freddie's ground. That's quite definite.' Kit tossed Aunty Fee a brilliant smile.

'No, to hang about those shops you seem to love so much.' There was an edge of sarcasm in Aunty Fee's voice. 'What about you, Elinor? Does a Big Mac, or a display of the latest watches lure you, like it lures Kit?'

'No, thank you,' said Elinor, brief and still dignified.

As if she'd choose to spend a day with Kit, things being as they were!

'You're not sulking, are you, Mouse, about you-know-what?' Kit inquired in an undertone.

'Certainly not.'

'I'll buy you a present,' he offered sweetly.

'Don't bother. Aunty Fee's bought me quite enough.'

'Are you sure you won't come?' Aunty Fee asked her. 'It'll have to be a major expedition. I'm running out of everything with you three here – not that I mind. And more snow's forecast.'

'She'll need me to help with the shopping bags,' Kit explained.

'I'd rather stay here,' said Elinor.

A solitary day should offer the chance of seeing Tom and Susanna again, and discovering more about who they were. And maybe she'd find a way, too, of showing Kit he'd been wrong.

An hour later, she watched the others drive away. It was bitterly cold, and the sky lay like iron along the ridge of the hills, but Elinor wasn't going to let the weather put her off. She would find Tom and Susanna – and then, all at once, she realized she hadn't the faintest idea how to contact them. They had always appeared at a time of their choosing, not hers.

She felt devastated. Had she stayed behind for nothing? No, somehow she *would* discover them. The valley seemed the most likely spot, so she put on her new boots and skiing jacket, and walked slowly down the hill, softly calling their names.

Nothing happened. The tray was still propped against the wall; the black river dashed past the stepping stones and the remains of the old holly grove; but that was all, and it was much too cold to hang about waiting. She collected the tray, and climbed back up to the Mill House, baffled.

They were still around, the ghosts. She sensed them as soon as she opened the door. They lurked in the shadows, projecting gloom and despair along the hall, and up the stairs. They caught at her – but she couldn't catch at them. It was as if a veil no thicker than a spider's web cut her off from them, and she couldn't break through it. She shivered, half tantalized, half frightened.

The day stretched before her, as grey and leaden as the sky. She wished that she'd gone with Kit and Freddie and Aunty Fee.

Idly, she crossed to the dressing table, and picked up

the old watch she'd left lying there. She stroked the comforting smoothness of its gold case. It almost seemed to have some message for her, though she didn't know what. She balanced its friendly weight on her palm, and then, for the first time since the night of the party, dug her fingernail into the crack, to prise up the lid.

There was the creamy face with its Roman numerals. There were the slim, arrow-headed hands. Once more she tried to move them, by twisting the knob, but they remained stuck, condemned to rest for ever at 6.20. Or 18.20, if you used a twenty-four hour clock.

1820!

That was the date Uncle William had given her; the date when the mill was still working. Suddenly Elinor remembered all the times she'd gripped the watch tightly, in anxiety or alarm. When she went into the Mill House for the first time, and shrank from the other guests; when she'd gone down alone to the candlelit party; when Freddie had scared her by going too close to the river. On each of those occasions she'd clasped the watch, and now, she realized breathlessly, each time she had done so, ghosts had appeared. Susanna had startled Mum by the staircase, and then materialized in the sitting room, seeking help. Tom had come down to the river to make his bridge.

So that was the link. Elinor felt a sharp twitch of fright. A power she didn't understand had fallen into her hands, and she was uncertain, even afraid, of how to use it. For the first time she wondered if the smooth gold watch might be dangerous.

But one thing mattered above all, and that was to find some way of convincing Kit about the reality of the ghosts. Taking a deep breath, she squeezed the watch, very gently, wondering what would happen this time.

A mist seemed to thicken through the room, cold and choking. It was still her room. The door and window were in their usual places, though a fireplace had mysteriously appeared in the wall. There was no fire in it, and the room was like the inside of a fridge, with patterned frost blurring the windowpanes, and a bitter draught snaking over the uncarpeted floor.

People moved in the mist; voices clamoured. Elinor's heart raced, as those hidden presences crowded in on her again, burdening her with their ancient distress. She nearly let go of the watch, but, forcing herself to be brave, she strengthened her grip.

The swaying mist cleared. She saw Susanna, seated on a wooden chair by the window, a bundle of sewing in her lap. Her long hair fell untidily over her shoulders. Her fragile hand, holding the needle, moved rhythmically, monotonously, to and fro. Elinor watched, half mesmerized by the glinting needle. Susanna stitched on and on, in a bare, bleak room, with snow humped on the window ledges, and frost shrouding the panes.

A tear fell down Susanna's cheek. She brushed it away, glancing up for a moment at the veiled window. Her clothes looked as uncared for as her hair. The collar of her long dress was all crumpled and a button was missing from the cuff. She seemed the focus of the stifling dreariness which filled the air. Elinor wanted to reach out to her. She tried to move towards Susanna, but something barred the way. She struggled to push it aside, but a dreamlike helplessness numbed her arms, and Susanna sewed on, out of reach, and unaware of her.

Suddenly, other figures came into view. Three children were tumbling about on the floor, fighting over a heap of toy building blocks. Two girls sat at a table with a jigsaw puzzle between them, and they too were arguing over every piece. These children seemed better dressed than Susanna. Spoiled darlings, Elinor thought indignantly, observing how combed, and curled, and frilled they were. But, as they quarrelled, and hurled down their bricks with a clatter to the floorboards, they seemed as unhappy as Susanna did. Wretchedness stirred and swelled in the comfortless room.

'I want to go out!' whined a boy of about seven, throwing his bricks into a corner.

'You know you can't, Arthur,' snapped one of the jigsaw girls; 'not in the snow.'

'I want to. Susanna, when can we go out?'

Susanna, stitching away, didn't reply. She seemed hardly to notice the tiresome children.

'It's beastly dull,' complained Arthur. 'I hate being stuck indoors.'

He knocked over the tower the smaller boy was building, and then joggled the table, spilling the jigsaw pieces. The nearest girl leaped up in a fury, and boxed his ears. There were howls all round.

'Mamma said you were to keep us quiet,' the eldest girl told Susanna priggishly.

'I'm busy making this shirt for your father,' Susanna replied distantly.

'Can't you do two things at once?' the girl sneered.

'Don't expect that, Mary!' her sister exclaimed. 'Susanna will do as little as she can get away with – unless it's for her precious Tom!'

'I'm afraid you're right, Lydia,' said Mary. Clearly, it was easier to agree over Susanna than their puzzle. 'Yet an orphan like her should be grateful to Papa and Mamma for their kindness. And stop that noise, Charlotte!' she yelled, for the little girl on the floor was shrieking as Arthur pulled her hair.

'He's taken my bricks!'

'Give them back at once, Arthur.'

'Shan't!'

'I'll kick you!' screamed Charlotte.

'Go on, then. I'll only kick back.'

'Oh, don't fight all the time!' cried Susanna suddenly, her voice sharp with despair. 'You've all got so *much*!'

In her mind's eye, Elinor saw the mill children. No doubt Susanna was seeing them too.

'How much have you got, Susanna?' demanded little Charlotte pertly.

'Oh, she's got nothing,' said Mary.

But Susanna's hand stole to her pocket, as if she was concealing something precious.

'My bricks!' the youngest boy howled.

Arthur had knocked them down a second time.

Like an old record stuck in a groove, the squabbling resumed. Rage, frustration, misery, swirled darkly round. There were slaps and shrieks. And it was as cold as a tomb!

Unable to bear it a moment longer, Elinor dropped the watch.

CHAPTER EIGHT

The watch fell from Elinor's hand, and plopped on to the eiderdown. Yes, it was the old-fashioned blue eiderdown, belonging to Aunty Fee, which Elinor had been using for the last few nights. She was sitting on her bed, thoroughly depressed by the dismal scene she had witnessed. Indeed, her heart positively ached for poor Susanna, isolated among that quarrelling tribe of cousins.

Eddies from the dark, ghostly past beat round her still, desperate to draw her back. Faint cries quivered on the far edge of hearing. Elinor couldn't stand them a moment longer. Thrusting the watch into her pocket, she jumped off the bed, and ran downstairs. Television might be a distraction.

It wasn't. She knew it wouldn't be, as she flipped the channels. Cartoons projected lurid colours; old movies offered smooth heroes and flirtatious heroines. But the ghosts crowded them out. They surged through the sitting room, dominating it with their unseen presence. Their voices drowned the competition from the television.

'Tom! Tom! We must get away.'

'How can we? Be reasonable, Susanna. We've no money—'

'You'll be too old to train as a doctor if you don't go soon. It's so wicked to keep you here! Oh – I'm so unhappy, Tom. If only there was someone to help you – but there's no one.'

Sobs shivered like snowflakes in the air, melting as a new altercation rose.

'The children need more food, Uncle, when it's so cold. A bucket of soup, sent down from the house at mid-day—'

'Why, in God's name, should I feed them? I pay them, don't I?'

'Very little.'

'Go and mend that pulley, Tom, and stop interfering, or you'll get no dinner yourself.'

An advertising jingle momentarily swallowed the talk, and then Elinor heard Tom again.

'They must be fed, Susanna, in this weather. They're weak with hunger. Oh, why can't Uncle William compare them with his own children? You'd think any human being would feel intolerably guilty, coming home from the mill, and finding those plump cousins of ours, gathered round the table with their spoons in their hands, when the mill children have barely a crust.'

'Uncle William isn't a human being.'

'We must do something ourselves, Susanna. I've been thinking. You've got Father's gold watch, haven't you? If we sold it to buy bread—'

'No, Tom! No! Not Father's *watch*. You've made *them a safe way to cross the river. Isn't that enough?*'

Her misery engulfed the shadowy old sitting room.

Elinor flew back to her bedroom, and dropped the watch into a drawer. The torments of the past were driving her crazy!

From the window, she saw that snow was falling again. She hurried down to Uncle William's study.

'We'll have to keep the drive clear, or Aunty Fee'll never get back,' she blurted out.

'Good thinking! You do what you can, Elinor. Sorry I can't help, with my heart.'

He looked over his glasses at her, and then back at his papers.

Elinor was grateful to have the shovelling to occupy her. The snow soaked her new jacket, but hard work kept thoughts and phantoms at bay.

'Well, you have done a good job, darling!' exclaimed Aunty Fee, sailing in later, with bagfuls of shopping. 'All the way home I was wondering if we'd stick, and there was the drive, beautifully cleared.'

'How's Mum?'

'Lots better. They say she can come out the day after tomorrow, if there aren't any setbacks. So, after all this shopping, it looks as if you three won't be here much longer. I'll put the extra bread in the freezer. You've no idea what a hit Freddie was.'

Freddie was smiling, bright-eyed and halo-haired.

'I sang to the ladies in Mum's ward.'

'You're joking!'

'I'm not. One of them had seen me on TV. She said our choir was the nicest Christmas programme.'

'You're bound to get a few nutters in hospital,' remarked Kit, trailing in last of all, with fewest bags.

'Why d'you say that, Kit?' demanded Aunty Fee.

'He doesn't like me singing,' stated Freddie.

Elinor rushed in, as usual, to smooth things out.

'It's only that Kit's not terrifically musical. I'm not, either.'

Kit's heavy-lidded stare hardly offered the thanks she might have expected. 'Tactful as ever, Mouse! I'm a touch more musical than you, I think. But you get funny ideas about things, don't you?'

Yes, thought Elinor suddenly. And one funny idea is that I have to walk on eggshells to keep you happy!

'Tell me about your singing, and about Mum,' she said to Freddie. 'I can be putting things away while I listen.'

Kit stalked off, alone and annoyed.

They linked up later by the sitting-room fire. The strange murmur of the burning logs, and the sharp glint of flames reflected on the holly leaves, kept Elinor's nerves quivering. The watch might be upstairs, but that didn't exorcize the presences which inhabited the rooms.

'I did buy you a present, Mouse, like I promised,' announced Kit, lounging in with a paper bag in his hand. He smiled brilliantly, to show she was forgiven.

Elinor peeped inside the bag.

'What is it?' asked Freddie.

'A sugar mouse, I think,' said Elinor.

She took it out. It had a string tail and thread whiskers, and it was green. Elinor dropped the mouse back into the bag.

'Don't you like it?' inquired Kit.

She shrugged, imitating him; imitating too, a nonchalant tone of his. 'I'm not mad about sugar mice.'

He couldn't have looked more astonished if the sugar mouse had jumped out of its bag, and bitten him.

'Aren't you?' were the only words he could manage.

'No. And don't play tricks with me, Kit. I've more important things to think about.'

He recovered himself. 'Obviously. Spooks, I suppose.'

She didn't answer, for what Kit mockingly called the spooks seemed very near. Somewhere behind her, maybe at the window, Tom remarked anxiously, *'There are perils in this snow!'* and Susanna moaned, *'Nothing goes right, Tom. Nothing!'*

Elinor jumped round, willing them to reveal themselves to Kit, but they chose to remain invisible.

'I don't mind eating the sugar mouse,' said Freddie hopefully.

Uncle William appeared, all jovial smiles. 'What about a game of Snap? I don't think you'll see anything out of the window, Elinor. It's as black as pitch, and snow's still falling. The river'll be a raging torrent when this lot thaws.'

'Isn't it a raging torrent already?' asked Kit. 'It was when Elinor and I looked at it, three days back.'

She noticed he said 'Elinor'. She'd rattled him. Well, so what? She'd meant what she said about his tricks. But, as Uncle William had pointed out, it was no use looking out of the window. Tom and Susanna weren't there. She sat down at the card table.

'I haven't crossed the stepping stones yet,' said Kit. 'I'll have to do it before we go home.'

He glanced at Elinor again, waiting for her reaction. All her life, she'd responded as he wanted her to. Alarm, horror even, was clearly expected of her now, but she couldn't bother with it. She picked up her cards in silence.

'Crossing those stepping stones would be foolhardy in the extreme,' said Uncle William, laying down the seven of clubs.

'What do you think, Mouse?' He was dead keen to needle her now.

'Snap!' was her only answer, as she turned over the seven of hearts.

CHAPTER NINE

Later in the evening, Kit came to Elinor's bedroom in his pyjamas.

'I'm worried about you, Mouse. I am, truly. You've changed so much these last few days. Is it because you've got this mad thing about seeing ghosts?'

'It isn't mad. There *are* ghosts here, all over the place.'

She spoke fervently, for, as soon as she'd opened the door of her room, the icy atmosphere which had caged Susanna and her quarrelling cousins had overwhelmed her again; and, though they weren't visible, a sense of their ancient bitterness came seeping out from behind the wallpaper, and under the carpet.

'D'you know what you're doing, Mouse?' Kit demanded. 'You're cutting yourself off from me. You've never done that before.'

She read in his face a real fear that she was slipping out of his control; that cords which had bound her to him all her life, were breaking. He was angry and alarmed – and placatory.

'I bought you a sugar mouse,' he said.

Wearily, Elinor screwed herself up for one last effort. It was important; and if only Kit would understand and believe her, she would love him as much as Susanna loved Tom – which was saying quite a lot!

'I don't mean to be against you, Kit, but, you see, things are happening to me that have never happened before. I tried to tell you yesterday, because I wanted to share it with you. I still do, more than anything, if you'll let me. But the fact is that I *do* keep getting into contact with the people who lived in this house and valley back in 1820. Cross my heart! They're all round me, and they're growing stronger and stronger. I can't blot them out—'

'Oh, yes,' he interrupted, cold again. 'The mythical Tom and Susanna, and that ogre, their Uncle William. Yes, I heard all you said in that rather wild way yesterday, and when we were searching so crazily for the non-existent stable you'd dreamed up. But it's a load of nonsense. It is, isn't it, Mouse? If you could tell me you've just been pretending – that you've trapped yourself in a sort of mad fantasy that's got out of hand – I won't blame you. I'll –' he was racking his brain for the right bribe – 'I'll go sledging with you as much as you want when we get home.'

'Go sledging!' cried Elinor. 'What's the point of that?'

'Don't be so dense!' he snapped. 'I'm trying to get you off this hook you've impaled yourself on. There you are, sinking into a great big, stinking bog of lies and make-believe—'

'A bog or a hook? Can't you decide?' Elinor was as angry as he was. 'And the ghosts aren't – they most definitely *aren't* – lies and make-believe.'

'Aren't they? Prove it then – *Mouse!*'

He stared challengingly at her, but she stared back, straight into his eyes.

'OK,' she said. 'I will.'

Aunty Fee seemed half inclined, next day, to take Elinor with her to see Mum.

'Kit had his outing yesterday,' she said. 'You were left here all by yourself.'

'I could have gone,' Elinor pointed out truthfully. 'And Kit didn't get to visit Mum.'

'You're a nice girl,' said Aunty Fee.

Something in her tone hinted that she preferred Elinor to Kit.

'Not specially nice,' Elinor contradicted quickly. 'Anyway, there's something I want to do here with Freddie.'

'Ghost-hunting?' murmured Kit, to no one in particular, raising an eyebrow.

Elinor didn't reply.

But that was, of course, her plan. As soon as Aunty Fee and Kit had gone, she turned eagerly to Freddie. He was fiddling with his Lego, and looking bored.

'Freddie,' she said, 'would you like to see something interesting?'

'OK. What?'

'A proper waterwheel, down in the valley.'

'Is there one?' he asked, surprised.

'I think so.'

The watch was in her pocket. She was nearly sure it would operate for Freddie as well as herself, since he had definitely seen Tom on the river bank, and heard ghostly voices. Today she would, if things worked out as she hoped, show him something really impressive. Then he could describe it to Kit – and that would be the proof.

They ran and slid down the hill. Elinor gripped the watch tightly, and there, strung between the holly trees, which had thickened into the old grove again, was Tom's bridge. It was no more than planks, lashed together to make a swinging path across the black waters. Snow lay crusted along it, but it looked far safer than the icy lumps of the stepping stones.

'See that bridge?' said Elinor. 'D'you remember the boy who rigged it up?'

'Yes, of course. He had a brown coat. Why?'

'I might want you to tell Kit.'

He looked surprised, but didn't question her. 'Are we going over the bridge?' he asked instead.

'No. The watermill's on this side of the river.'

She led the way upstream, threading between the clutching holly boughs.

The noise alerted them to the mill, before it came in sight round a curve of the river; the thrashing thud of a wheel, revolving in a fast current of water. They hurried forward past the cottages, which crouched, in pathetic huddles, close to both banks, and reached the walled mill yard.

'Here we are!' said Elinor, thankfully. 'Now for the wheel.'

She went boldly through the gate, into the yard. Threatening clouds had darkened the sky, but a yellow gleam of candles through the mill windows guided them along a slippery path. There were sounds from inside the mill as well, a whirring and a rattling, but they were half drowned by the crash of the wheel.

Then, round a corner, they saw it.

'Wow!' cried Freddie. 'It's *awesome*!'

The wheel towered as high as the mill; a great hoop of wood, with spokes radiating to a rim that was not smooth, but broken into broad, flat, overlapping blades. They caught the river current, which forced them round, driving the wheel; and all along the eaves of the roof above hung huge, jagged icicles, formed by the ceaselessly flying spray.

'It's unbelievable!' gasped Elinor.

It was indeed quite a sight.

'What's the wheel for?' shouted Freddie, above the racket.

'To work the machinery inside the mill, Uncle William said.'

Freddie was prancing with excitement. 'D'you think we could see the machines?'

They both scanned the wall of the mill. Its high windows were above their heads, but a low door stood ajar in a corner, and Freddie darted over to it. He beckoned eagerly to Elinor, giving a thumbs up.

'It's OK,' he mouthed, as she joined him. Ordinary talking was impossible, so close to the thundering wheel and the clattering machinery.

Elinor peered through the doorway. She blinked,

rubbed her eyes, and peered again. She was looking into a vast room, which stretched the whole length of the mill. Candles, bowing and guttering on the windowsills, gave out a glow of light, but it was dimmed by the haze of flying fluff which filled the air. She heard people coughing and spitting as if they were choking.

Down the centre of the room ran close rows of bobbins, as tall as the men who were tending them. A ramshackle arrangement of fly-wheels and pulleys overhead kept them spinning round. They clacked and rattled as they whirled, and, all the time, everything – the floor, the candles, the bobbins – was shaken up and down by the pounding of the waterwheel.

It was a moment or two before Elinor made out the children; tiny shapes in the candlelit gloom. As Uncle William had said, there was a child for each worker – a piecener, that was the word Uncle William had used. The pieceners stood close to the workmen, twisting and smoothing the yarn as it ran on to the bobbins, with an automatic, see-sawing motion of their thin hands and arms. Barefoot, semi-naked, they worked like machines themselves, staring vacantly into space, and occasionally turning their heads to cough, and spit on the roughly-boarded floor.

Or not so very occasionally. The child at the end of the row nearest to Elinor and Freddie was in a dreadful state, racked with paroxysms of coughing which nearly brought him to his knees. He let go of the thread, and the workman cuffed him, shouting angry words, which were inaudible through the clamour. The child resumed, eyes closed, hands working mechanically, and then doubled up again, in a fresh coughing fit.

Suddenly Tom was beside him, with a pail of water and a jug. He dunked the jug, flinging water into the air and over the floor, dowsing the fluff, so that, just for a moment, there was a patch of clear air, and the child could breathe. He opened hollow eyes, in a face like a skull, to grin weakly at Tom, and Tom grinned back, playfully flicking a few drops at him, to cheer him up. Then he moved away, along the line of bobbins, and the flying fluff was back, enveloping the child.

Freddie's sharp elbow dug into Elinor. 'That was the boy at the bridge!' he shouted.

Elinor nodded; and though she was in a state of shock over the appalling mill, she felt a touch of relief that Freddie really was seeing the things she was seeing, and would be a perfect witness for Kit.

A bell clanged, ending the day's work. The machinery shuddered to a halt. There were normal sounds of voices, and hurrying feet, as workers grabbed coats and caps, and made for the main door, halfway down the room. An old woman scuttled round, blowing out the candles.

'Oh, they must be glad it's over!' breathed Freddie. 'Are they ordinary children, like us?'

'I suppose so,' Elinor answered slowly. It was hard to feel any likeness to the stunted creatures, who were hobbling out into the snow. She shrank against the mill wall, not so much afraid of being seen, as ashamed of her own and Freddie's healthy bodies, and warm, bright clothes.

The sister and brother she had seen under the holly trees crept past with their little lantern. Others followed. They weren't laughing and chattering, as they had done when they helped Tom with his bridge. They were too tired. More than one was marked with trickles of blood from a beating.

'It's awful!' gasped Freddie.

'Here!' Tom was in the yard, among the limping children. 'I've got some bread, to help you home.'

He took a lump from his pocket, and tore off pieces, pressing them into weary, listless hands.

'Cheer up! A mouthful of bread will keep you going. And mind you take care on the bridge.'

'Come wi' us, mester Tom,' one child begged.

'If you like.'

He hoisted the smallest on to his shoulder, and strode towards the gate of the yard.

'Nobody won't drown now. Not like Isaac,' a small voice piped, as they headed for the trees.

Immediately, another sound caught Elinor's ear; a sob of exhaustion and pain. She looked back quickly through the doorway. The child with the bad cough was on the floor, half under a great bobbin, sprawled out as if he had no strength to move.

One glance, and Elinor flew out into the mill yard.

'Tom!' she shouted. 'There's a child left behind.'

She didn't know if he would hear her. Susanna was the only ghost with whom she had actually communicated, and some unseen barrier might have held her apart from the rest.

But Tom responded – to something, even if it wasn't to her. He put down the child he was carrying, and looked back.

'Where's Sammy?' she heard him say.

A moment later, he had swung past Freddie and Elinor, and into the mill again. Instinctively, Elinor followed, halting on the threshold, and gazing into the great room, where the fluff was sinking down in a greyish dust, and the boy cried and choked under the bobbin.

In a trice Tom had fetched water. He raised Sammy, holding the mug to his lips, but it was no use. Sammy was too weak to swallow. His head lolled against Tom's shoulder, and Tom's hand moved rapidly to his heart, to check that it was still beating.

'What's going on?'

A rough voice bellowed through the mill. Uncle William, the millowner!

'It's Sammy Johnson,' said Tom. 'He's ill; seriously ill. Consumptive, I think. He hasn't got the strength to go home.'

Uncle William advanced heavily, and poked Sammy's leg with his boot.

'He's a goner,' he announced briefly.

'He's not. He'll revive if he takes some water. I could put a drop of brandy in it. There's some in the counting house, I think.'

'He's having no brandy!' William Kershaw exclaimed. 'He's not worth the money.'

Gently but fast, Tom laid Sammy back on the floor, and sprang to his feet. He faced his uncle, blazing with anger.

'How can you be so cruel? He's not a machine. He's a child, the same age as Arthur.'

Roused to equal fury, William grabbed a stick, which was leaning against the wall, and struck out—

CHAPTER TEN

Wham! A snowball crashed into the back of Elinor's neck. Thud! Another hit Freddie on the shoulder.

'Ha! Got you!'

They leaped round.

From the hillside above, Kit was attacking them with a battery of snowballs. A dozen more were piled on the wall, rounded and ready for use.

'Stop it!' shouted Elinor. 'What d'you think you're doing?'

'What d'you think *you're* doing?' he countered; but at least he lowered his arm.

'Looking at the mill.'

'Which mill?'

Even before she had glanced quickly back over her shoulder, Elinor knew it would be pointless. The mill, with its great wheel and ghostly people, had vanished. The black river bounded and gurgled past a flat, untrodden stretch of snow.

'I've never seen such a pair of mega-goofs as you two,' Kit sneered; 'staring into space with your mouths open.'

Freddie rushed to defend himself. 'There *was* a mill, and its wheel was going round. And there *were* people. And there was a bridge, under those trees, by the stepping stones.'

'Show me, then.'

Kit slid the last few yards down the hill, a mocking smile on his face.

Elinor gripped the watch, but nothing changed. The power of Kit's derisive unbelief was stronger than the fragile power of ghosts and lost time. The mill and its workers had been sucked back into the dark chasm of long ago. Thoroughly dejected, she followed her brothers along the river bank, under the withered hollies.

'I know it'll be there. We've seen a bit of it before,' said Freddie. And then, blankly, 'It isn't!'

'You don't need a bridge,' drawled Kit, 'when there are stepping stones. Anyone could cross them. I'd cross them myself – only I think we should get straight back to the Mill House. You especially, Mouse. There's something seriously wrong with you.'

'What d'you mean?'

'Exactly what I said. It's bad enough, making up stuff about the past to seem important, but persuading Freddie to believe in things that aren't there – you must be off your head! I shall suggest Aunty Fee takes you to a doctor. Freddie probably needs one as well. Look at him!'

Elinor wrenched her attention from Kit to Freddie,

and her heart sank still further. He stood on the bank, frail as a grasshopper, miserable, bewildered, and shivering.

'Freddie, you're frozen!' exclaimed Elinor.

'What do you expect, when you make him stand up to his boot-tops in snow for hours on end? You'll get some flak, Mouse, if he starts with pneumonia,' warned Kit. 'Come on. It's crazy lingering by imaginary bridges, when Freddie should be back beside a fire.'

Still Elinor tried to justify herself, useless though she knew it was. 'You aren't psychic, Kit. Freddie and I are. And Uncle William can tell you all about the mill.'

'Precisely!' His voice was sickeningly triumphant. 'Uncle William innocently gave away all sorts of details to you, so that you could make up things for you and Freddie to pretend to see.'

He was maddening. Elinor appealed to Freddie. 'Can't you describe to Kit what we saw in the mill; the bobbins, and the children, and Tom, and all that? It'd prove we weren't inventing things.'

But Freddie's face had tightened into a mask of wretchedness. Tears dribbled down his cheeks. 'I don't know what we saw,' he wept.

'Nothing at all! I was right,' crowed Kit.

'You've no idea how totally crazy Mouse has been,' said Kit.

They had found Aunty Fee and Uncle William in the kitchen. Warm and cosy after the snow, with Aunty Fee boiling the kettle, and Uncle William taking biscuits from a tin, and nibbling one with a contented murmur of 'Chocolate!', it should have been blissful. But it wasn't, not while Kit was producing his string of accusations about the sightings of imaginary ghosts.

'Worst of all,' he finished, 'Mouse seems to have got it in for you, Uncle William. She's actually been pretending that you're in the habit of beating people up.'

He favoured Elinor, and then the others, with his arrogant stare.

Aunty Fee poured out mugfuls of tea, splashing some on the table in her haste.

'Take your tea into the sitting room, please, boys. Give them some biscuits, William. Elinor, you stay here.'

'I could tell you more, Aunty Fee.'

'Probably you could, Kit, but I've heard enough. Off you go.'

She hustled them out of the room.

'Now, Elinor darling.' And, at the kindness in Aunty Fee's voice, Elinor's eyes prickled with unexpected tears. 'Sit down. You look exhausted. We quite agree with you, don't we, William? This house *is* haunted.'

'Have you seen the ghosts too?' asked Elinor in surprise.

'No, we haven't. Oh, we've felt them, me more than Uncle William. But they've stayed outside our range of vision. They aren't interested in us. You see, it's an odd fact that ghosts are often drawn to young girls like you; girls who are particularly sympathetic, and sensitive, and receptive. And they can choose little boys like Freddie, who share some of the same characteristics. Somehow, Kit's not the right type for them.'

Again that edge in her voice suggested that Kit was not her favourite of the three Trenthams.

'So it's not Kit's fault,' said Elinor; in spite of everything, rushing automatically to his defence.

'Not seeing ghosts certainly isn't his fault. As for refusing to believe in them . . .' Aunty Fee shook her head. 'You're a super sister, Elinor. He doesn't deserve you. All we want to say is—'

Uncle William took over. 'Steer clear of the ghosts. Forget about them. You're going home tomorrow.

Obviously we believe you've seen them, and felt their strong presence, but it'd be best to put them behind you. Very firmly.'

'They're only phantoms,' said Aunty Fee, 'dead and gone years ago. There's nothing you can do now to change their sorrows.'

'No.'

And Elinor yawned. She felt incredibly tired after so much stress and emotion.

'Why don't you go and lie down on your bed for a bit?' Aunty Fee suggested. 'Uncle William'll keep the boys happy.'

'We might try Black Maria!' Uncle William exclaimed. 'I'll get the cards.'

Elinor shut the door of her room – and the ghosts pounced on her out of the shadows, gibbering, clamouring, but invisible; engulfing her in all the rage and despair that had been trapped in the valley for nearly two hundred years. Being acknowledged at last had given them strength, and their sheer force nearly stunned her. She stood frozen and aghast, desperately wondering what she had let loose. They were calling her, drawing her to them, demanding her response with a strident urgency of which she couldn't make any sense.

If she could throw down the watch – but, as she tried to snatch it from her pocket, they beat against her so fiercely that she needed both hands to thrust them away, and clear a space of air in front of her face, before she choked. Mist and darkness enveloped her. She was powerless.

'I *want* to help you!' she screamed. 'I just don't know how. Why don't you tell me? Susanna!'

There was no answer; only the terrible anguish of the past, let loose upon her in the gloom.

She flung herself in the direction of the bed, intending to roll up in the eiderdown, and shut them out—

Only, it wasn't an eiderdown. It was Aunty Fee's cloak. She was wrapped in it, running out of doors into a blizzard that was almost a white-out. I must go, she found herself saying in her head to someone – she didn't know who. As if watching her own actions in a dream, she plunged forward.

Down the freezing hill she raced, while snow swept blindingly past her. It stacked up in mounds on the dark stone walls, and, as the holly trees came into sight, they were bent double, like crippled children, under the weight of it. Still the unseen forces drove her, willing her on.

Faintly, through the whistling wind, she heard a cry of fear. Or perhaps it was just the wind. The sounds twisted and plaited together, the wailing of the wind, and the increasingly shrill screams of human voices, while the trees creaked and groaned in unison.

She flew down the last steep slope, into the dark valley. The snow lashed against her, thickening into shapes that wavered, and flapped, and shrieked as they whirled past.

'The bridge! The bridge!'

They weren't just blowing shapes of snow. They were children, their mouths gaping holes of terror. Icy hands scrabbled at Elinor's face, and clutched her cloak.

'Help! The bridge!'

She crashed through the trees, and jerked to a standstill. Tom's bridge had collapsed under a mass of snow. Half of it still hung from the trees across the river, but the nearer half had fallen into the water, when the ice-coated ropes had snapped. It slanted like some grotesque, drinking animal, its head beneath the current.

And there must have been children on it when it fell; children who had added fatally to the weight of the snow. Horror-stricken, Elinor saw a cluster of small heads, bobbing in the rushing water. Arms like twigs thrashed and strained for rescue. But rescue was impossible. The waves were hurling them downstream, tossing them like driftwood.

'They were on t' bridge, six on 'em,' a child's voice moaned, and echoed around and around in her head.

Then the snow came down in a thick white blanket, hiding the tragedy; and, as it blew away, she found she was back in her own room, watching Tom and Susanna, but separated again by that unseen veil of cold.

A candle was gleaming above the old, lost fireplace, throwing light over Tom's rough brown hair, and bowed shoulders. He sat with his head buried in his hands, and Susanna knelt on the uncarpeted floor, with her arms round him, in a desperate attempt to give comfort.

'It wasn't your fault. You didn't know how heavy the snowfall would be.'

'I should have guessed,' he groaned. 'I should have got to the bridge early, to warn them.'

There was silence. Susanna clasped her brother, and shook with suppressed sobs.

'Six,' said Tom brokenly. 'Six on the bridge when the ropes snapped. And only one, poor Isaac, drowned from the stepping stones.'

'Don't think of it like that. And remember that Sammy Johnson was dying already. The river shortened his agony.'

'But I'm to blame, Susanna; to blame for all those deaths. I've blamed Uncle William for cruelty, but I'm far worse than he is. I'm a murderer.'

'You never meant—'

'What I meant doesn't matter. It's what happened that counts. Six deaths, Susanna, and I'm responsible for them all.'

He was sobbing too now.

'You'll do good again. I know you will,' cried Susanna.

Tom only shook his head. 'All I can do is give the money to see that those poor children have proper funerals.'

'How? We've no money at all.'

'No. But –' he pulled himself away from her, and began pacing up and down the room. 'There's Father's watch. You wouldn't let me sell it before. Now I must.'

Susanna shrieked, and her hand flew to the pocket of her dark dress.

'No, Tom! No! We mustn't part with it. It's all we have left.'

The candle guttered, and went out.

CHAPTER ELEVEN

Modern electric light blazed in Elinor's bedroom. The ghosts had gone, but Elinor lay rigid, her heart banging in her chest. The fallen bridge and the drowning children, the agony of Tom and Susanna; the pictures reeled endlessly through her head. She felt as if she was possessed by the ghosts.

She looked at her wristwatch, and discovered with amazement that it was nearly ten o'clock. Hours had gone by while she lived in the past. She'd been rapt away, or slept, through supper and long after it. Her head felt muzzy, and her limbs weak.

With a great effort, she took the old watch out of her pocket. Such an innocent-looking thing, its gold circle so smooth, and solid, and comfortable! Such an evil time-trap, dragging her away into the sorrows of the past. Aunty Fee had told her to put those sorrows behind her, but she couldn't while she carried around the watch that had once belonged to Tom and Susanna. And it would not let her go.

She must get rid of it.

Holding it lightly, she crept on to the landing. To her relief, there was a line of light under Kit's door. He was safely out of the way! The blackness round Freddie's meant he was asleep. Elinor stole past, and began to tiptoe down to the dimly-lit hall.

A creak of hinges below made her jump in alarm. She peeped over the bannisters, and saw that the door – the old, lost door she had gone through with Susanna on the night of the party – was visible, and ajar. A freezing wind licked through it, and on the threshold, touched by moonlight, stood Susanna. Her long hair streamed in the draught, her cloak fluttered round her, and she shivered, glancing back longingly towards the shelter of the hall.

'Oh!' A frail hand flew to her mouth to check the cry.

Elinor, who'd almost screamed herself, gripped the bannister rail. For a long moment, they gazed at each other. In the ghostly, greeny-grey eyes of Susanna, all the hopelessness which haunted the hall seemed to be concentrated. Then the door blew shut, with a crash. Elinor leaped down the rest of the stairs, and flicked on more lights. Susanna had gone, and the wall had closed up, as if no door had ever been there.

Uncle William and Aunty Fee looked up in surprise, as she burst into the sitting room.

'Woken up at last, darling?' began Aunty Fee. 'Why – what's the matter?'

Elinor was shaking like a leaf.

'I don't want this watch,' she said, trying to keep her voice steady, but failing miserably. 'I think it's making me see the ghosts.'

She held it out, and Uncle William took it.

'H'm. Early nineteenth century.' He prised open the lid, and examined the watch face closely, tried to wind the knob, failed, and remarked, 'An old crock, but handsome.'

'Where's it come from?' asked Aunty Fee.

'I found it among the stones in the bridge, where the road to Bellshill goes across the river. We stopped there, on our way to your party, and I pulled it out. I liked it at first, but now –'

And she launched into the whole story.

'It's the hands,' she finished. 'You see what they're pointing to? 6.20, but you can read it as 1820. That's why, every time I've held it tightly, I've gone back to the days of Tom and Susanna. No, don't try it!' she cried, as Uncle William's fingers folded inquiringly round the gold case. 'They almost seem to want me to do something for them, and I can't work out what it is. I've had enough of them. I don't want to have anything more to do with them. Not ever!'

Tears flooded down her cheeks.

Aunty Fee and Uncle William were angelic. With hugs and kindness, soup and toast, they gradually restored her.

'It's been a rough ride for you,' commented Uncle William, 'but it's fascinating to me. Sure you don't want that last piece of toast?' He took it. 'You see, all that you've said ties up, quite uncannily, with my research. Some children *were* drowned in the river in 1820, though I hadn't found out why; and William Kershaw had an unenviable reputation as a tyrant to his workforce.'

'I wish you'd burn your tiresome papers!' said Aunty Fee, with sudden sharpness. 'What's the point of digging all this up? I think it should be forgotten.'

'Historical curiosity, my dear,' said Uncle William mildly.

'I wish it could be forgotten too,' agreed Elinor. 'And I've had an idea. If I put the watch back in the wall, the ghosts might stop haunting me. Oh –' her voice dropped in dismay – 'but suppose another person discovered it. With the hands stuck at 1820, all that misery would just be recycled. It would start up again, and that would be awful for the finder, and even worse for Tom and Susanna. They can't want to go on living through it, time after time.'

'Good idea about putting it back, though,' said Aunty Fee. 'William, what *are* you doing?'

Uncle William was running his thumbnail round the circumference of the watch.

'Have you noticed this, Elinor?'

'What?'

'There's a second crack. I bet you can open the back of the watch, as well as the front.'

He wiggled his nail, and another lid sprang open. Underneath, in a circular cavity behind the watch-face, a mass of microscopic wheels, cogs and levers was meticulously packed.

'The works!' said Uncle William. '*Not* working, of course.'

'Can we start it?' breathed Elinor.

'Possibly, but I don't think we will. We'll just try and move the hands. Have you a needle, Fee?'

Aunty Fee produced one. Uncle William inserted the point into a cogwheel, and pressed. Almost imperceptibly, it moved. He turned the watch over, and they saw that the hands had passed, just fractionally, beyond 6.20. He resumed his work with the needle.

'It's twenty-five to eleven,' Aunty Fee told him.

'Ah, but I don't want the real time.'

'What then?'

'Let's bring it up to date. If the year 2000 is eight o'clock, I'll put the hands just before eight. That should scotch the ghosts. Bingo!'

He held out the watch, and Elinor saw that the arrow-headed hands were indeed pointing in new directions.

'What's the snow like?' Uncle William got up, and twitched back a curtain. 'No worse. Get your nice new coat, Elinor. We'll take a little trip to the bridge straight away.'

Ten minutes later, his car pulled up at the spot where Elinor had stood, listening to the river.

'I'll do it,' Uncle William offered. 'I'll stick in the watch so deeply that it won't be found for donkey's years.'

He climbed out, and was lost for a moment in the shadows by the bridge.

'Do you know,' he remarked, heaving himself back into the driving seat, 'it doesn't seem so cold. I wouldn't be surprised if a thaw was beginning.'

Elinor didn't answer. She was staring out to where, on the edge of the headlamps' beam, she had half glimpsed a slight, light figure, with long, pale hair, stealing away into the darkness.

CHAPTER TWELVE

On their final morning at the Mill House, Elinor was, once again, the last down to breakfast. She left her bedroom cautiously, every nerve on edge, to discover if she and Uncle William had exorcized the phantoms. Immediately, she was disappointed. No flitting shapes could be seen, no voices heard; but the presences, though lessened, were undoubtedly still there. The same dull misery leaked from the walls, and lurked in the shadowy corners.

It was indeed a sad house; sad even when the watch wasn't there. She should have guessed that, from what Aunty Fee had said.

She opened the kitchen door, braced for a sarcastic

remark about dormice, but none came. Kit ostentatiously ignored her. Freddie was chatting to Aunty Fee. Elinor sat down, and helped herself to cereal.

In spite of the lights, the kitchen seemed as gloomy as a prison. The bank rose steeply beyond the windows to the drive; the hillside beyond the bank. It struck her anew how the valley was a trap. It had trapped Tom and Susanna eternally, so that the moving of an old watch that had once been theirs, had no effect on them at all. But for her, at least, escape was near.

'What time are we fetching Mum?' she asked.

'We're to be at the hospital around 2.30,' said Aunty Fee. 'Uncle William's going to run your mother's car down, and I'll take mine. Then, if she doesn't feel like driving home, we'll take her, and come back here in my car.' Suddenly, she looked quite melancholy. 'I'm going to miss you.'

'We'll come and see you, lots of times,' Freddie promised.

'Or you could come and see us,' said Elinor swiftly. She wasn't going to return to the Mill House in a hurry.

Still Kit was silent.

'Do you know what day it is, apart from the day your mother leaves hospital?' asked Aunty Fee.

'Your birthday?' Freddie guessed.

'No. It's Twelfth Night. That means we take down all the holly and evergreens, and burn them. Could you three do it?'

'Of course we could,' said Elinor.

'I'll tell you one thing,' remarked Uncle William. 'The thaw's setting in.'

'But it's still so dark!' cried Aunty Fee.

'I know. But the temperature's rising.'

And all the time, Kit didn't speak. He didn't – as he once would have done – claim that he had predicted a thaw. He had no brilliant suggestions to make about the day's arrangements. And, when he looked at Elinor, he scowled.

At first, while they were taking down holly and ivy from the beams, and carrying it outside for burning, while they were smoothing out red ribbons, and rolling them up for next year, Elinor managed to keep away from Kit. But at last, just as she was perching on the top of a stepladder, prising out the tacks which held the now withered wreath over the fireplace, Kit came in – and she was caught.

He advanced to the foot of the ladder, and stared up at her.

'Where did you go last night, Mouse?'

Unprepared, she floundered. 'Where –? Oh, no-where.'

'Don't tell any more lies, Mouse. I happened to look over the bannisters, and I saw you leaving the house with Uncle William, at about a quarter to eleven. And then his car drove away.'

Somehow, it helped that she was looking down on him from above. He was dwarfed by the ladder's height; just a smallish boy, thrashing about in a situation beyond his control. All the same, there was no point in telling him what she'd been doing.

'OK,' she said. 'I did go out with Uncle William, but not very far. I dare say you heard us come back.' For she could imagine him, all too clearly, furiously alert for their return from an adventure he'd been left out of. 'But I'm not going to explain it to you, because you'd only say you didn't believe me. I don't blame you for that. I just don't want us to get into another silly quarrel. So please don't ask any more. We're going home today, and then it'll all be forgotten.'

'And you really think that's good enough, Mouse?' he demanded, his voice throbbing with anger. 'You think you can sit up there, all toffee-nosed, and tell me to mind my own business?'

'Yes,' she answered simply.

She felt his willpower struggling against hers, almost as if it was a living force, straining up the ladder towards her – and falling back.

'I hate you, Mouse!' he snarled, and he stalked out of the room, stiff as a poker with rage.

But I'm not a mouse, thought Elinor. I'll never be one again. She knew she had won some strange contest with him. All the same, her hands were shaking, and her knees felt like jelly. It was a few minutes before she was strong enough to finish unpinning the wreath, and totter down the ladder.

Uncle William had made a bonfire of holly branches near the garage. The flames leaped brightly, the blazing leaves crackled and popped, and snow melted into pools. As Elinor carried the wreath across, she saw Freddie dancing with delight, while Kit skulked sullenly apart.

'Look, Elinor!' called Freddie. 'Isn't it brilliant? I wish we had a guy. Where did you get all this holly from, Uncle William?'

'Those trees down by the river. They're rather poor old things, but I managed to lop off all this lot.'

'Oh!' exclaimed Freddie. '*Those* trees! We saw someone rigging up a bridge down there, didn't we, Elinor?'

Elinor hesitated, not knowing how to answer, and Kit suddenly came forward, still scowling.

'It'd be daft, having a bridge there; totally, utterly mega-daft. There are stepping stones, aren't there?'

'The stepping stones are dangerous,' said Elinor.

'Exceedingly dangerous,' added Uncle William.

'Huh!'

Kit's derision scorched like a bonfire flame. Elinor turned away, picking up scattered twigs.

'Anyway,' said Freddie, comfortably unaware of the tension, 'we won't have time to go down to the river again. And I don't mind. The hill's too steep.'

He kicked a straying branch back on to the fire, enjoying his braveness.

'Well, I must tear myself away,' said Uncle William, 'and check up on your mother's car. I squeezed it into the garage, so it should be all right, but we need to be sure it'll start. Dear me!' he went on, as he headed for the garage. 'The thaw's certainly started. Look how the icicles are beginning to drip.'

'It's not a thaw. The bonfire's melting them,' said Kit scornfully.

'At this distance? No, you're wrong.' He vanished through the garage door.

Every nerve in Elinor's body prickled. Even with her back to Kit, and her arms full of scratching twigs, she sensed his fury at being called wrong. Tension seemed to stretch between them, like taut wire; and then, out of the corner of her eye, she saw Kit beginning to run. Away from the bright fire and the Mill House he darted, and down towards the river, and the perilous stepping stones.

'Kit!' she shouted, and, flinging her sticks on to the blaze, she tore after him.

The snow on the hillside was no longer ice-crusted, but its softening surface was just as lethal. And she wasn't wearing boots. Her feet slipped in every direction, and once she fell to her knees, struggling up with sodden jeans, and wedges of snow under the tongues of her Reeboks. But Kit dashed ahead, and she had to follow.

She was fifty yards behind when he reached the bank. His bomber jacket swung and wove among the hollies. He knew exactly where he was going.

'Kit!' she yelled. 'Don't be mad!'

If he heard, he paid no attention. He came to the point where the stones ran out into the dark water, steadied himself, and jumped. Elinor, breaking through the trees, saw his feet skid as they landed, and his arms fly out for balance. And then he was upright and safe on a slushy-topped rock, with the river rushing past, behind and in front.

She didn't dare to call again, in case she startled him. She stood motionless on the bank, her blood turning to ice, and he jumped again, and, with a slide and a scramble, reached the second stone.

With terrifying vividness, images from the ghostly world overwhelmed her. She saw skinny, outstretched hands, and drowning heads sucked under the current. 'Oh – Kit –!' But he jumped again, and landed securely in the middle of the third stone. He knew she was there. He glanced back. 'Easy!' he boasted, and leaped again.

She saw him miss his footing, and scrabble frantically for the fourth stone. His body jack-knifed, his arms and legs flew out, and he crashed backwards into the surging torrent.

Elinor screamed at the top of her voice. 'Tom! Tom!' A faint answering splash broke through the roar of the water, as if someone had jumped, or dived, in. All the little icicles which fringed the branch Elinor was clutching, tinkled down into the river, but Elinor didn't notice. She was straining her eyes, through mist and flying spray, to where a brown head struck through the current towards the fair head that was Kit's, which rose, and was swallowed, and rose again, its face livid with terror.

Unable to look any more, Elinor closed her eyes. Suddenly, there was a splosh beneath her, and a crackle of breaking ice. Strong arms, Tom's arms, were holding Kit up, and he was shouting to her for help in getting Kit ashore. Together – yes, it must have been together; she could never have done it alone – they heaved Kit on to the snowy bank, gasping and choking, but alive.

'Thank you!' breathed Elinor. She could hardly believe what had happened. She looked down at Kit, struggling to his knees, and blowing water out of his nose – and then she looked round for Tom. But he was nowhere to be seen. He had gone, and taken all the unseen presences with him. Only the hollies stood round her, witnesses of a final, ghostly drama.

'Kit, are you OK?'

She found herself hugging him, as she hadn't hugged him for years, getting soaked as Kit hugged her back, shivery and weak as he was.

'Let's get home quick. You must change your clothes.'

She hauled him to his feet, and hurried him up the hill, as fast as she could.

'Who was it – who helped me? I felt someone in the water,' Kit gasped.

'It doesn't matter. You're safe now. Oh, Kit, *thank goodness* you're safe!'

They'd almost reached the house. Wisps of smoke still curled from the bonfire.

'Elinor,' said Kit tremulously – Elinor, not Mouse! –'don't tell. I feel so stupid – *was* so—'

'I won't,' Elinor promised. 'We'll just creep quietly inside.'

And, somehow, they did. She smuggled poor, quivering, water-logged Kit up to his bedroom, ran him a bath, bundled his wet clothes into the carrier bag which had brought her culottes, and made him a hot drink, all without encountering anybody.

Kit emerged from the bathroom, dry and warmly dressed, with the colour restored to his cheeks.

'Thanks, Elinor,' he said.

The words might be short, but they were meant a thousand per cent.

'It's OK. You'll find some coffee in your room. I'm going to pack.'

She opened her bedroom door, just as the sun, for the first time in their stay, broke through the clouds, and touched the Mill House with gold.

86

CHAPTER THIRTEEN

The speed of the thaw was incredible.

Seconds after that first gleam, the sun powered strongly through the clouds, spreading sapphire where all before had been grey. Melting snow gushed down the hillside in sparkling rivulets. Icicles ran like taps, and an optimistic blackbird whistled from the shiningly clear ridge of the roof, as if spring had come.

Elinor hovered at her bedroom door, sensing, yet hardly daring to believe in, the miraculous transformation that was taking place. The house felt empty, light, washed clean. She moved slowly along the landing, and down the stairs, searching and listening, but the ghosts who had lurked there had gone. No more Tom; no more Susanna. They were winter phantoms, and their winter, at last, was over.

What had really happened, she would never know. Maybe the ghosts had been jerked forward in time, when Uncle William altered the hands of the watch, but Elinor preferred to think they had been set free when Tom's wish was fulfilled, and he had saved Kit from the dangerous waters. She and – surprisingly – Kit had together laid them to rest.

They drove off to collect Mum, crossing the now familiar hump-backed bridge where the whole adventure had started; Elinor with Uncle William, the boys in Aunty Fee's car. The river, swollen by melting snow, roared beneath them.

'I pushed the watch in pretty deeply,' Uncle William remarked. 'I wonder how it got into the wall in the first place?'

Elinor thought of Susanna's ghost, flitting away from the headlamps' beam last night. It would be nice to confide in Uncle William, as long as she didn't mention Kit and the stepping stones.

'I believe Susanna put it there,' she said. 'I think it belonged to her father; that it was the last relic she and Tom had left of him. Tom might have wanted to sell it – maybe to pay for the funerals of those poor little children who were drowned. But Susanna couldn't bear to let it go. So I think she hid it, well away from the Mill House, but in a spot where she could find it again some time. Though it looks as if she never did.'

'You seem to have acquired a good deal of information about her,' Uncle William observed quizzically. 'What an advantage to be psychic! I hope you'll take to history when you grow up. Your gift could come in very handy!'

Bellshill Hospital was enormous, and crowded with visitors. There was a struggle to find spaces in a distant carpark, and then a lengthy trek to Mum's ward. They passed through light, modern wings, and then on to the dark, cramped halls of the original Victorian hospital, the centre from which the rest had spread.

Aunty Fee flew purposefully along, trailing them all in her wake.

'I wish I'd got my skateboard,' grumbled Freddie.

'Surely there's a lift,' sighed Uncle William.

'It's not much further,' Aunty Fee encouraged them. 'This way.'

Their voices drifted back down a staircase to Elinor, for, in the old entrance hall, she had jerked to a sudden, amazed standstill. What was that bust, standing on a narrow column in the corner? Or rather, *who* was it? As she stared, a lopsided smile she remembered seemed to meet her across yards of nonslip tiling.

'Kit!' she hissed.

The others went on, but he turned round.

'Kit! Come here. You *must*!'

'What's wrong?'

'It's Tom. Come and look.'

Kit – the new Kit, or was it the Kit of long ago? –

bounded back down half a dozen steps, and joined her. They whisked over to the corner where the bust stood, and, together, read the inscription on a plate fastened to the column.

'Thomas Kershaw, founder of Bellshill Hospital, 1803–1870. Thomas Kershaw left home to find work as an assistant to a physician in a poor district of Bellshill. After qualifying as a doctor, he continued to practise in the same quarter of the town, and founded this hospital in 1840, to care for the sick and needy.'

'Oh!' breathed Elinor.

She couldn't help smiling, because it was so marvellous to know that Tom had escaped from the trap, and become a doctor after all.

'Who –?' began Kit.

'The Tom who lived at the Mill House. Susanna's brother.'

'But look how long ago he died!' exclaimed Kit. 'It's yonks. Elinor, he wasn't – was he –?'

'One of the ghosts? Yes, he was.'

'I never saw them,' said Kit regretfully. 'But, the funny thing is, I kind of feel there's something a bit familiar about his face.'

'You might have seen him this morning,' said Elinor.

'*This morning?* Elinor, you don't mean that – when I fell off the stepping stone –?'

'Tom rescued you? Yes. Yes, I think it was Tom. I didn't see him very clearly either, but it *felt* like him. And it was the sort of thing he wanted to do.'

Kit let out a yelp of excitement and triumph. Elinor had never seen such a grin of pure delight on his face.

'Then I've seen a ghost too! Wow! I though it was just you and Freddie, and not me. I was so *jealous* of you. You wouldn't believe how much – well, you would. But then, in the end, I didn't just see him. He *rescued* me. Honestly! A ghost! It's sensational!'

'I think you'd better cool it,' Elinor warned him. 'You're going right over the top. People'll think you've flipped your lid.' It was fun to be able to say that to Kit, her superior brother, and know that he wouldn't mind at all, but would just go on grinning at her.

'Come on,' she urged him. 'Tom Kershaw's in the past now, and I'm dying to see Mum.'